RIPCORD

A BILLY BECKETT NOVEL (BOOK 3)

BY
SCOTT PRATT

WITH KELLY HODGE

Scott and I talked often about the potential of the Billy Beckett series. The inherent drama of the sports world — its heroic nature and endless intrigue — appealed to our sensibilities as writers. The various games could serve as compelling backdrops to all kinds of fictional adventures, and in our minds, Billy was a worthy protagonist.

Scott helped me plot a way forward at a time when I was uncertain about the project. He then took an active role in developing storylines and characters that resulted in co-authorship. I've been honored to share that cover space with him. The plan was to produce three books together and gauge readers' interest in the series, see if Billy should press on. I'm pleased to say that he will.

Tragically, Scott left us far too early, less than five months after his beloved Kristy, my only sister, lost her long battle with cancer. He was a man of unique personality and talent, and I will always miss his friendship, insight and encouragement. Adding to his fine catalogue of fiction, which has been warmly received and reviewed for many years now, has been a bittersweet task without him.

As *Ripcord*, the third book, is released, I trust Scott would be proud of the effort. Thank you to all of his faithful fans, and new readers alike, for your support.

— K.H.

This book, along with every book I've written and every book I'll write, is dedicated to my darling Kristy, to her unconquerable spirit, and to her inspirational courage. She lost her 11-year battle with breast cancer on June 23, 2018. She fought like a lioness to her last breath. I loved her before I was born, and I'll love her after I'm long gone.

-Scott

PART ONE

CHAPTER ONE

The night was late, but Russell Mann was still wired. He had walked off the arena floor just a few hours earlier to a standing ovation and scattered chants of his increasingly popular nickname. The most spectacular performance of his career, arguably the best in franchise history, would surely raise eyebrows around the league. He was becoming a next-level star. An *all-star*. *Super Mann!*

Let the haters chew on that a while.

Russell had stopped at a trendy new nightspot in Park Lake-Highland to celebrate with friends, ending his self-imposed ban on drinking in public. He even picked up the tabs of everyone sitting at the bar, to more applause, before heading home after midnight.

He should have been a satisfied man, ready to get a good night's sleep and build on a seminal achievement. A quadruple-double — thirty-one points, thirteen rebounds, ten assists, ten steals — could sway opinions far and wide in the basketball world. There had been only a handful ever recorded in the league, and none in the last twenty-six years. Few players would dare to dream of such a feat.

SCOTT PRATT

The timing couldn't have been better for Russell. His current contract in Orlando was about to expire, and behind the scenes other suitors were already lining up to bid for the services of the gritty six-foot-eight forward. There was little doubt that he had earned a huge raise, perhaps a nine-figure deal in the new NBA economy. The stat-stuffing outburst against Charlotte would only bolster his credentials.

But for the moment, Russell had more pressing concerns on his mind.

As the clock ticked toward two, he was bothered and pacing around his airy home in the Windermere community. He couldn't forget what happened earlier at the nightclub, an old acquaintance from the Bronx named Blue Warren — one of his guests at the game, in fact — disrespecting him that way, feeding a potential girlfriend sordid details about his past. Even from a distance, he could see it on her face. *That look.* She was so shaken that she excused herself and took a Lyft ride home. And now she wouldn't answer his calls.

Had Blue forgotten that the big man was always keeping score?

Such disrespect wouldn't be tolerated in Hunts Point, and it wasn't going to be tolerated here either. The air had to be cleared. The more he thought about it, the angrier Russell became. And when he was angry and intoxicated, all bets were off.

He snatched his phone from the table and dialed T-Bone, the most trusted member of his entourage, who had dropped him at the house less than an hour earlier. Russell wanted to see Blue Warren again. Soon.

"Tell him he has to have one more drink with us before he heads back," Russell said. "We'll pick him up at the motel."

Russell walked quickly to the bathroom, found the brown glass vial tucked away in the back of a drawer, and tapped out a small pile of powder on the granite countertop. He stared at himself in the mirror. His eyes were vacant, his features expressionless — so unlike his game face.

Basketball purists appreciated the full scope of his skills, from the sweet mid-range jumper to the suffocating defense. But raw intensity is what set Russell Mann apart, made him one of the most polarizing figures in the league. It percolated from deep within, threatening to boil over every time he stripped off his warm-ups and stepped on the court.

The only evidence now of the fire burning inside that big body was a trace of perspiration on his forehead. He closed his eyes and took a deep breath.

Against all odds, he had escaped the unspeakable violence of his youth. He had been able to manage the beast to get this far, into this rich Florida air. At twenty-five, his future suddenly looked brighter than anyone back home could ever have imagined.

Yes, he was a long shot. Even the grandmother who raised him figured Russell would never live this long. He was his own worst enemy. Couldn't let any slight go. Constantly looking back. Always finding reasons to be offended. *Dangerous.*

Three years in the NBA spotlight hadn't changed any of that.

He peeled a bill from the folded stack of hundreds in his jeans pocket, rolled it up, and snorted the powder. Then he walked down the hall to the closet and grabbed a black box from the top shelf.

A text pinged in on his phone; it was from his agent. *Just saw the stats. EPIC! Keep pushing. Talk tomorrow.*

Russell suddenly felt a tingling on the back of his scalp. He smiled and opened the box. Inside was a Glock 17 pistol, one of several weapons he kept scattered around the house. He popped in the loaded magazine and cradled the gun for a moment before wrapping his long fingers around it, like he had done so many times before. There was a knock at the door.

He slid the Glock into a Magic duffle bag, took another deep breath, and eased back into the darkness.

CHAPTER TWO

Blue Warren had one hand in his hoodie pocket and was leaning against the building smoking a cigarette when the black sedan pulled up outside the lobby. He took one last, long draw and flipped the butt into the shrubbery.

"I didn't know you boys were still riding around," he said, sliding into the back seat. "Thought you went home, Russell. It's late and I already got a hell of a buzz. Where we goin'?"

There was no answer. T-Bone glanced in the rear-view mirror and began to drive out of the motel parking lot. Russell kept his eyes straight ahead.

"Russell, I thought you'd be tired from putting up all those numbers tonight. That was hard work … you carried the team. Man, I never seen nothing like that."

Blue was a short, stocky man with close-cropped hair and a prominent scar across his forehead. He had been in a few scrapes, to be sure, but in the neighborhood he was known more as a talker with an easy smile. His personality was an asset at times and a liability at others. He didn't always know when to shut up.

"You enjoyed yourself?" Russell said, opening the pint of whiskey that T-Bone had brought. He took a sip and passed it over his shoulder.

Blue followed with a big swig. "Hell, yes. Made that long drive from the city worth it. May feel different when I wake up in the morning and have to go back. Right now, real good. T-Bone, I thought you said we gonna stop for a drink, maybe get a bite. I'm hungry."

"Not many places open this time of night, not places you'd want to be. We'll just ride."

Russell glanced back. "You don't like the bottle? Just like home, only better. Tell me again what's going on in the hood. It's been a while."

"No reason to come back, right? Hunts Point don't change much, except, you know, losing cats. Andre went down a couple of weeks ago. You remember — big guy down the street, used to play linebacker in high school. Was always stoned as hell out there on the football field. Got crossed with the Henchmen. Wrong place, wrong time. Shoulda known better."

"What about Dimeco?"

"Man, he's hooked bad. Don't even look like the same dude, probably lost thirty pounds. Wouldn't be surprised to see him go next."

Russell reached for the bottle, took another drink and passed it over to T-Bone. "Go that way," he said. "Away from all this."

"You lucky to get outta that mess, Russell, I'm telling you. Always knew you had the game. Was saying to my brothers before I drove down, Super Mann is one of the best ballers ever to come out of the Bronx."

Russell managed a half smile. "*One* of the best?"

"Okay, *the best*. Tonight, no doubt. Damn quadruple-double. I'll always remember that." He laid his head back against the seat, smiled, and stretched his legs across the floorboard. "You know, lot of people said you wouldn't make it out. Thought you couldn't keep your shit together; guess it just ran in the family. Man, you were trouble every which way."

Russell gritted his teeth and took a deep breath. Blue would be the unfiltered fool, right to the end.

"They didn't think I was smart enough? Who?"

"No, not that. Didn't mean that. Just, you know, takes a certain kind of man to make a living in the NBA. Can't have all the craziness around."

Russell looked over at his driver, who was showing signs of concern. "What about you, T-Bone? You think I'm man enough?"

"Sure, Russell. Three years in the league speaks for itself."

"Take this road," Russell said. T-Bone turned onto state route 441 toward Apopka and kept driving until the city lights behind him had begun to fade.

"How many times you think I left home, just to keep Gran safe? Who had my back? *Nobody*. All I had was ball."

"You were a big target, Russell. Lot of people wanted to take a shot. You had to fight your way out."

Russell grew more agitated. "Damn right. Had to fight the whole way. People don't show the proper respect. Didn't then, and still don't. I'm still fighting."

"You gonna sign a new deal soon, and it's all good. You in a new world. Maybe it's time to chill a little bit, Russell."

"Would that be your advice, Blue? *Just chill?* You think I can forget all that's happened? Don't work that way."

"Okay."

"Tell me again, Blue, what you said to Sasha."

"Your *girlfriend?*" He turned sheepish. "She asked me how I knew you, and we just started talking. She seemed interested, kept asking more questions. Guess I should have stopped. Sorry she left."

"You know, I been trying for weeks to get her out. She works downtown near the arena. I'd seen her eating lunch at this place, gave her a ticket to the game and talked her into going to the club. Then she ends up having to hear your shit." He slammed his fist on the dashboard, causing both of the other men to flinch. "Why?"

"No offense, Russell. Take it easy. She wanted to know."

"And you just couldn't stop talking, making me look bad. She won't even answer now. All because of you."

"Sorry, Russell."

"You know, that really pisses me off. Best game in Magic history, and then that. Couldn't even enjoy it for one night. You've always rubbed people wrong, Blue. I should have remembered when you wanted a ticket. You don't show the proper respect."

Russell turned up the pint and shook his head. Blue bit his lip; finally, he had nothing to say.

"Go right and slow down." T-Bone did as told. There were no lights now, and he noticed Russell fidgeting with the duffle bag near his feet. A look of dread appeared on his face.

"Up here," Russell said. "Pull over."

CHAPTER THREE

"**W**e weren't really in love."

The words, strung together so simply, so matter-of-factly, still stuck like Velcro in the back of Billy Beckett's mind. Rachel was right, of course. She was beautiful and smart and fun — always a breathtaking romp in the sack. But they weren't in love.

Ultimately, that's what it came down to.

Billy leaned back in his seat and gazed out the window of the private jet. His thoughts were racing. The last two days in New Orleans had triggered a flood of memories, good and bad, but they hadn't produced Bradley King's daughter. She was still unaccounted for, out there somewhere.

It was time to go home.

The questions hung over Billy. *What would Rachel do next? And how should he prepare?* He had no good answers.

The strain showed on the faces of both passengers as the young co-pilot stepped from the cockpit and announced that they had been cleared for departure. Moments later the jet engines began to whine. The flight was bound for Knoxville, Tennessee to deliver Billy, and it would continue on to Charleston, South Carolina with King, who lived on Isle of Palms.

The mood in the cabin was far different than the day the men headed off to the Gulf Coast together. They had hoped there was a chance to get to the bottom of this, to track down a woman who had no obvious reason to disappear in the first place. Now there was only a fresh sense of resignation.

Finally, Billy spoke up. "I'm sorry, Bradley, for what it's worth. This has only gotten more complicated."

King glanced over and nodded. He was disheveled, tired. The polo shirt and khakis he wore were badly wrinkled, like he had slept in them, or tried to. His silver hair was uncombed, and the bags under his steely blue eyes hung heavily.

Gone was the carefully crafted image — the tall, swaggering developer who had raised the family name to new heights with a string of projects along the South Carolina coast, from Myrtle Beach to Hilton Head. The CEO of King Ventures simply looked like a worried father.

King clicked his lap belt and pulled it tight. "Her mother is going to be devastated," he said. "Losing all touch like this … we just don't understand. I thought we had a chance to get her back, or at least talk to her."

Billy was caught in an awkward position. He felt responsible, somehow. At the same time, he was a victim of Rachel's whims himself. He shouldn't have to apologize.

"It's still hard to believe," he said. "Everything was good. Then it all went to hell."

King shifted uneasily in his seat. Rachel hadn't been home more than a couple of weeks after leaving Tennessee. She had said little about the kidnapping to her parents, but they could tell she was depressed. Still, they expected her to bounce back and move on, like always. Rachel was resilient.

"She said she needed some space, wanted to get away and clear her head," King said. "She had a new position in the company waiting, and it was perfect for her. You know how sharp she is with real estate. I was hoping maybe she'd help me run the business some day. But she never gave it a chance. Just got in her car that afternoon and drove off."

Billy's eyes narrowed. The words were chilling, and painfully familiar. Rachel had left him, too, with little warning. Just got in her Mercedes coupe one day and drove off, putting their mercurial relationship in the rear-view mirror. Near as he could tell, she never looked back for long.

He had seen her only once since — at his brother's funeral in Sevierville, three days after John committed suicide. They spoke for a few minutes after the service, standing in the rain at the cemetery. She apologized. And then she drove away again.

Not long after that, she disappeared.

"Seems like she just wiped the slate clean," Billy said. "No money trail. No credit card transactions. No contact with old friends. Nothing."

"She had access to money, plenty of money. She has the means to live just about any way, or anywhere, she wants."

"Tell me what's going through her mind at this point, Bradley. That's what I can't grasp. How did we get here?"

King shook his head. "This isn't how she was raised. She's always been a free spirit, but it seems like her mood swings had gotten worse. Her mother and I had to deal with that when she was younger. We did the whole therapy thing and she gradually pulled out of it. By the time she got through college, I thought most of the troubles were behind us. Rachel had a toughness about her. She was ready to take on the world."

"She's definitely a free spirit," Billy said. "I never knew where that would take us from day to day, which was part of the intrigue. There were always bumps in the road, times when she'd go her own way, but we were able to smooth them out."

"Everything changed after the kidnapping. Something just snapped."

King flashed back to their last conversation on the phone. Rachel said she was visiting friends in New Orleans. Thought she might go down to the Caribbean for a while and would be back in touch. That was it.

Her father had surprised Billy with a call a few months back, asking him to try to contact Rachel and reconnect the family. The men used to be friends, but it was more than that. King's financial backing had helped the sports agent get his fledgling business off the ground in Knoxville, even helped him secure the big house on the Tennessee River. All he wanted was for his daughter to be involved, well cared for, and happy.

Billy got nowhere when he tried to reach her. The trail was cold. Even her closest friends had lost touch.

It was a busy time for Billy Beckett Enterprises, which was immersed in contract talks at the end of the football season, so he moved on. The months passed.

He hadn't given Rachel, or the cryptic messages, much more thought — until a few days ago.

There were two handwritten notes, one sent by mail from New Orleans and another mysteriously left at his Knoxville home. On his bedroom pillow, no less. *It's Not Over Yet.* What did she mean?

That was the last word.

"She missed you," King said. "It was obvious. She invested more in that relationship than any other she'd ever had with a man. She didn't want it to end."

"Bradley, she's the one who packed up and left. It wasn't my idea."

"She must have reconsidered. There were doubts. I think she really did love you."

"Then why didn't she just call and talk to me?" Billy said. "How did we end up here, with what we know now? How did Rachel get involved with the mafia?"

CHAPTER FOUR

The night had begun as an ill-conceived rescue mission. It ended up being a bloodbath.

Two of Frank Romano's henchmen were gunned down in the New Orleans warehouse where Jarvis Thompson, the college football star, was being held. Two others, including Romano's own son, died outside near the gates as the place burned to the ground.

What no one realized at the time was that Rachel had been in the car with Paul Romano. She had left Isle of Palms to be with him, and she was standing somewhere in the shadows, watching, when it all came to a head.

Billy was still trying to come to terms with the knowledge as he settled into his seat for the flight home. The betrayal ran deeper than he could have imagined. And now this twist: Rachel toying with him again, from a distance. Was she flirting? Or threatening?

"You know she's always been unpredictable," King said, breaking the silence. "She's got that wild side; probably came from her mother."

"I understand that better than most, but what we're learning now is something else. If she's stalking me …

I don't know *that* Rachel." Billy stared intently at her father. "Why would she turn on me like that, Bradley?"

The troubling questions had to be confronted, again and again. *Why would Rachel abandon her loving parents? Did the young woman who had everything simply snap? Could she now be dead herself?*

King laid his head back and looked out at the cloudless sky. The whisper of the Cessna Citation Bravo was a steady sound track in the cabin.

"We never knew anything about Paul Romano, never met him. He was just a guy in a band she liked to go and listen to when she was home. A guitar player, for God's sake. To find out that his father was this notorious mobster in New Orleans — and that he ended up being involved, and dragged my daughter along for the ride … it just blows my mind."

Billy rubbed his face and exhaled a deep breath. He knew where the conversation was headed. Again.

"Of course, this all goes back to you," King said. "You were the one Frank Romano was fixated on, the one he wanted to hurt. He used his son to get to Rachel, knowing she was close to you. She was a pawn. Or at least it started out that way."

"I didn't know, until it was too late … I hate to keep saying it. Rachel told me at the cemetery that the father had called her, blackmailed her to leave Knoxville, get away from me. She never mentioned Paul until I confronted her about it. She said they were just friends. Obviously, it was more."

A private investigator her father had hired found evidence that Rachel was living in New Orleans with

Paul Romano. The neighbors saw her come and go. Tall, dark and mysterious, they called her. The kind of woman you didn't easily forget.

There also was the police probe of the warehouse fire. A source told a reporter for the *New Orleans Tribune* that a distinctive compact was found in the floorboard of Paul Romano's vehicle, not far from where his lifeless body was sprawled out on the pavement. Made of fine Amboyna burl, the lid had the initials RAK — Rachel Ann King — in pearl inlay. It had been a birthday gift from Rachel's mother, Elaine. The cops never made the connection.

"There's no doubt that she was there that night," Billy said. "The question is what happened after that. And where is she now?"

The thought lingered for several minutes before King spoke again.

"She could show up anywhere. Maybe she'll just come home on her own. Her mother and I won't rest until she does."

King pressed deeper into the headrest. Exhausted, he closed his eyes and drifted off, alone with his rambling thoughts. He didn't stir again until the pilot's voice crackled from the sound system. "We're beginning our descent into Knoxville, gentlemen."

The Cessna landed and taxied toward the executive terminal. Billy straightened up in his seat, stretched his legs, and gathered himself for the short drive home.

"You know, Bradley, I owe you for everything you've done for me," he said. "But I've got a lot on my plate right now. I can't worry any more about Rachel. I've lost enough sleep over her already."

"I understand. And I appreciate you taking time to help me look for her. I won't call again unless something changes. Be careful, and we'll keep praying that this nightmare is over soon."

The jet finally rolled to a stop. The co-pilot stepped out of the cockpit and dropped the exit stairs. Billy stood to pick up his travel bag and laptop and looked down at Bradley King one last time. There wasn't much left to say.

They shook hands and Billy descended to the tarmac. He strode slowly toward his silver Escalade in the small parking area, tossing his belongings in the backseat. Once inside, he pulled out his cell phone and scrolled down the favorites. The voice on the other end brought a smile to his face.

"Claire, I'm back."

CHAPTER FIVE

Claire Bosken struck a relaxed pose in the doorway of his office early the next morning, a steaming pot of coffee in her hand.

Billy had gotten used to starting his days with a shot of caffeine and a conversation with her. Both were stimulating in their own way. After a few days away, he was anxious to catch up.

"So, no sign of Rachel?" Claire said, filling two mugs on his desk. She stirred in the sugar and a splash of cream, just the way he liked it.

Billy pushed his chair back and shook his head. "She was gone, but we know she'd been living in New Orleans up until a few weeks ago. People saw her around. Now, who knows?"

"I'm sorry. If there's anything I can do …"

He waved her off. "You've done enough, and so have I. Let's get on with more pressing issues. Sit down. I want to know what's going on."

Claire strolled past him and took a seat on the couch facing his desk. The distinctive notes of her Opium perfume trailed in her wake. The fiery redhead could light up any room. If the exotic face and full figure didn't command attention, the bubbly personality most certainly did. Billy had a healthy respect for her all the way around.

"Anything good happen while I was gone?" he said.

"No, it's been pretty quiet. Jackson and I were hoping you'd be able to put this thing with Rachel behind you, one way or another. You know Jackson; he's really been out of sorts over it for weeks. The way it's been looming … I know it's starting to play with your mind, and we don't need that."

"She was always hard to understand, but this is surreal. She waded into some deep shit in New Orleans, hooked up with some bad guys. I don't know why, or how it'll end, but her parents are crushed."

"And you're right in the middle of it again." There was that playful smile. "For a sweet Southern boy, you seem to find a lot of ways to complicate your life. You're a magnet for trouble, Billy Beckett."

He could always trust Claire to bring levity to any situation. It was a natural reflex. She enjoyed the teasing, the give and take, especially with men.

In the aftermath of the Jarvis Thompson kidnapping, which sent some clients scrambling for cover and caused all sorts of image problems for the company, her management style had served Billy well. BBE had rebounded in a big way.

"Trouble just seems to find me," he said. "I don't know why. I'm not looking for any."

"The unassuming sports agent. Fun and games, right?" She smiled again. "That's too easy. We both know better."

At times like this, Billy found himself fighting hard to maintain perspective and stay on track. He didn't need any added entanglements with his new business partner — a married woman at that. But there was a complex history between them.

Claire was the forbidden fruit, tempting and within arm's reach, and he had to resist any urge to take a bite. It had been that way for years.

"I was just trying to help Bradley," he said. "I feel bad for him and Elaine. They've lost their only child. Regardless, I told him that I'm moving on. I can't afford to spend any more time out chasing the wind. And that's what Rachel seems like right now; I can feel her but have no idea where she's coming from. I don't expect to hear from Bradley again until something breaks."

"What *do* you expect? This is like some Fatal Attraction thing with his daughter. I think she's lost her mind."

"Weren't we supposed to be moving on to more pleasant topics, here? Rachel will turn up eventually, hopefully alive and well. I don't wish her any ill will, but she has some serious issues to resolve. She's flirting with disaster."

"Maybe she's just living off the grid somewhere. You said she always liked to go to tropical places and disappear. She could be with the surfer crowd in Hawaii for all we know."

"No, she's closer than that."

Billy tried to dismiss the possibilities that had been rolling around in his head. The images of the dark-haired beauty were still vivid. His imagination could run wild if he let it.

"Anyway, we've got a business to run here," he said. "So let's move on. BBE is cranking, and I'm thankful for that."

Claire had officially been Billy's partner for only a few months. She deserved it, after stepping up and over-seeing the company's affairs while he was still trying to clear his head. Truth be told, she saved the operation.

The new collaboration was already yielding results. More athletes were willing to listen to their sales pitch. The top-shelf players were still largely out of reach, but the roster was growing. BBE was a viable agency with charismatic leadership.

Their success was nothing new. Billy and Claire were a good team from the start.

Their relationship had begun more than a decade ago at the University of Tennessee. They were classmates in law school and used to study together occasionally. Even enjoyed a beer or two to unwind down on The Strip when time and circumstances allowed. But it never got much closer than that.

Claire Miller was already dating a guy named James Bosken, and they ended up getting married right out of school. He became one of the most prominent attorneys in Knoxville. She was one of the most talked-about women in certain circles, a formidable attorney in her own right.

Billy had packed his bags and worked in corporate law in Atlanta for five years before coming home and starting his business. By then, he was heavily involved with Rachel King, a woman with a powerful vibe of her own.

She was a heart stopper for a man several years older, a former volleyball star at the University of Georgia who commanded the limelight. She was at ease in any setting, especially around athletes. "One of my best business assets," Billy liked to call her. Rachel followed him back to Tennessee and became a fixture at the big house on the river. Whether it was love or not, they were happy enough.

Now she was in the picture again, in some distorted way. The last few days had only made it more difficult to understand.

"I don't want to keep bringing it up," Claire said, "but why do you think Rachel is doing this? She already had you to herself once. You guys lived together off and on for years."

He nodded. "Something changed. Eventually we'll find out what."

"I didn't know her well, but I never thought she was good for you. Always seemed like a schemer to me."

Claire almost blushed at the sound of the critique. It was more spirited than she intended.

Billy smiled and raked his fingers through his brown curls. Tall and athletic, he had a way of connecting with most everyone who came in contact with him. Women were easily charmed.

"That's kind of the way things played out at the end with my brother," he said. "Maybe it's somehow coming back into play — the cocaine and the lies. She couldn't be trusted. Not much doubt now."

"I'm just going to tell you what I've been saying for the last year or so: keep moving forward. Don't look back. Great things are happening for you."

"Happening for both of us. Now, let's get down to business. *Please*. You said yesterday that you had something on your mind."

"A couple of things, actually. I've been thinking about them a lot for the last few weeks."

With that, Billy propped his feet on his desk and took a big gulp of his coffee. "Shoot."

CHAPTER SIX

"Let me start small," Claire said. "What would you think about tweaking the identity of the company, giving us a little different profile?"

Billy scowled. "*Tweaking the identity?* What does that mean?"

"The name just seems a little cumbersome the more I see it. *Beckett Bosken Enterprises*. Kind of stuffy, especially to young athletes from the South. And that's been the bulk of our business. I think we can come up with something more attractive."

"More attractive? How about Bosken Beckett Enterprises?" Billy said with a chuckle. "Or Backwoods Management. *Gonna take care of y'all.*"

"I'm serious here."

"Okay, what do you have in mind?"

"How about Élan Sports and Entertainment? ESE. Energy. Style. Enthusiasm. Has a little more cachet."

"What is it, *French?* And these young athletes from the countryside will know what élan means? I'm not exactly sure I do either. Hold on a minute. *Entertainment?*"

Claire looked at him nervously. "That's the main thing I've been thinking about. We have the organization in place now. I think we can do more."

"More of what?"

"I think we should expand our reach. Musicians, performers ... there are real opportunities to get into the entertainment industry. Like I said, it would be a new identity of sorts, a rebrand. But with the same personal touch that has made the business what it is. We can never lose sight of that."

Billy sat motionless, a bit dumbfounded. He began to slowly rock back and forth in his chair as he tried to grasp the concept.

"So we've got this fresh momentum going with the athletes. People in all the major sports leagues recognize our name now; we're a legit agency, a real player. And we're not only going to change our name, we're going to distract ourselves by chasing after a client base we know nothing about."

"Not true," Claire said. "I've been spending a lot of time on this. Take Nashville alone, right down the road from here. There's not a deeper talent pool in the country for musicians and songwriters. And more people from television and film are moving there all the time. As you're aware, I have very good contacts in that area, so I know what I'm talking about. There's so much going on ... it could be a huge opportunity."

Claire grew up in Belle Meade, an affluent Nashville suburb, and always had friends who were well connected in country music circles. These days it wasn't just country; performers from all genres were flowing into the capital city. It was a hot spot nationally.

"With a few breaks, I think we could have an immediate impact," Claire said. "It just takes the right package to make the connections."

"And that package would be *you?*"

"Both of us, but I could get the ball rolling. There's a friend in Nashville, an attorney, who I've been talking to. David Noel. He'd like to be part of the organization on a commission basis. He's young and sharp, knows the ropes, and is friends with a lot of musicians. You could keep your main focus on the sports side, and I think Jackson is ready to step up and be a more valuable player there. He's another one who's young and sharp. You get the picture: ESE has a lot to offer."

Billy quit rocking in his chair and sat silently. He had become a player rep because of his lifelong love of sports. He related to athletes, their aspirations, triumphs, and struggles. He didn't know much about the music industry and was skeptical that newcomers could get in the game quickly, considering all the competition between talent agencies. Nashville was thick with them.

It was going to take more than a slick pitch from Claire to change his mind.

"You know what we've gone through to get to this point," he said. "I thought we were sunk not long ago, and I was about ready to quit. But you kept pushing, kept me going, and we built things back up. And now here we are, in this great position to take advantage of all our sports assets. Just look at the NBA. The salary cap is about to make another big jump, and there are going to be more commission dollars out there. Russell Mann alone is going to be worth millions to us. We've got all kinds of things going that will pay off soon."

Claire let him finish.

"I guess what I'm saying is, Why rock the boat? Let's just go with the flow for a while, enjoy the ride. We deserve it, right?"

Claire stood to build her case with that bright smile, her blue eyes sparkling. She was always a passionate advocate for whatever position she staked out. This time Billy was the jury.

"What is it you're always saying — no guts, no glory? And now you believe the company should just sit back and enjoy the ride? That's not our style. What happened to that famous sense of adventure?"

"It hasn't gone anywhere. I just want to make the most of what we've built here. These athletes deserve the attention to detail that we're known for — our full attention and energy. They're putting their money and trust in us. We're essentially guiding their lives."

"I'll tell you something about athletes," Claire said. "They love musicians. And musicians love athletes. They follow each other. If we can bring them together under one roof, it's a perfect match. And I know exactly where to start."

"Where?"

"I don't want to say right now, but if you'll agree to let me explore this, on behalf of ESE, I promise you won't be disappointed. We can take things to another level."

"You keep saying ESE."

"Or whatever we agree on. Let me work on it and I'll present you a formal proposal. We'll meet again soon. It'll be your call."

Billy rubbed his chin for a few seconds and finally nodded. "Fair enough," he said, "but it'll take some major convincing. For now, though, I have to get back to the grind. Things are piling up, and I'm supposed to be in Orlando at the end of the week."

Claire walked back over with the coffee pot to refresh his mug and smiled again. "No guts, no glory. Just think about it."

CHAPTER SEVEN

Meetings with Russell Mann tended to leave his agent with mixed emotions, equal parts excitement and dread. This one was no different.

With the NBA season winding down, Billy eagerly anticipated setting the parameters of a new contract for the prized forward — one that everyone was comfortable with regardless of how the negotiations played out. If Russell remained with the Magic, he'd likely receive top dollar. And he was comfortable in central Florida. The smart bet was that he'd stay put.

But it was up to Russell, and it was hard to tell what he was thinking at any given moment. Reading him was always a challenge.

Billy rang the doorbell and looked around the property. It was a nice place, very nice, in fact, but not over the top for a star athlete whose earning power was on the rise.

He was formulating a plan that would pay Russell more than ninety million dollars over four years — guaranteed money in the NBA. Even after thinking about it for a while, the figure still almost took his breath. A four percent commission would be worth more than three and a half million dollars over the life of the contract. And if all went well, the next contract would be even richer.

Likeable or not, Russell would become one of Billy's most important clients once he signed. Aside from the financial windfall, new doors would open for the agent in professional basketball. *Success breeds success,* he liked to say. A deal like this would be a sure sign that his firm was coming on strong.

Billy couldn't see anyone stirring inside the home and walked around the porch. It was late morning on a typically hot, sunny day. The Tudor-style mansion in Windermere, Florida, an exclusive golf community dotted with lakes, stood tall on a quiet cul-de-sac. An elaborately landscaped fountain and koi pond was the focal point of the property in front. The backyard had a kidney-shaped pool, gazebo and entertainment area that bordered an exclusive golf course.

Like a lot of pro athletes, Russell was paying for far more living space than he could ever use. In his case, the opulent lifestyle didn't match the man. For starters, he had never once played golf. Never even held a club in his hands, at least not for the purpose of hitting a ball.

His entertainment tastes leaned more toward intense video games. A large den in the house had been converted into a theater, with four plush recliners surrounding a gigantic TV screen. An Xbox One X console sat in the floor nearby. Russell spent most of his time there.

Down the hall was another spacious room with a white Steinway baby grand piano. Nothing else. No matter that Russell didn't play the piano, and didn't know anyone who did. He wanted a white piano.

Billy had long since given up trying to rationalize the tastes of pro athletes in their twenties. With their money, they could do most anything they pleased. At least Russell had resisted the urge to buy a fleet of expensive cars. He only had three in his four-car garage — Mercedes SUV, Lexus sedan, and Aston Martin sports coupe — though he was shopping for a speedboat to fill the other spot.

The agent went back to the front. After the third ring, the big man finally appeared at the door. He opened it, mumbled something, and ambled down the hallway toward the kitchen.

"Good to see you, too," Billy said, stepping into the expansive foyer. "I hope you're a little quicker on the court tonight."

No response.

"The Knicks used to be your favorite team, right?"

"Yeah, they sucked then and they still suck. Haven't even had a winning record in five years. Won't this year either. Ought to be embarrassed to have New York on their jerseys."

The exchange was a reminder of how quickly even small talk could get bogged down in negativity with Russell. Billy wanted to steer the conversation in a positive direction and keep it there. There was no reason to be negative. Not today.

"The question is where you guys will finish. You're right in the hunt for a playoff spot. It's been a while. If you finish strong, that's going to help with the contract talks. Could help a lot."

Russell mumbled again and lurched toward the refrigerator. He looked a little ragged as he grabbed a

Coke and glanced out the back window. A landscaping crew off in the distance appeared to be constructing something in the corner of his neighbor's yard.

There was an uncomfortable silence in the kitchen. It was typical. Billy had never bonded with the kid from the Bronx like he had with most of his other clients, and they both felt it. Russell tended to keep his distance — withdrawn, dark and sullen, suspicious. He was emotionally scarred in ways Billy couldn't understand.

The agent preached family, needed to feel a deeper connection. Russell wasn't like family, and some days didn't seem like much of a friend either. In fact, he was almost uncoachable when it came to personal relationships. And that impacted his potential to become a transcendent star in the NBA, unlike others who seemingly shined in every situation.

Russell had grown up on the mean streets of New York City, a bullying, paranoid youth raised by a grandmother who had little control over him. He bounced from one school to another, carrying the bitterness with him. He was hard to love, and not many people even tried to get close.

One of the few was Derek Woodson, his AAU coach. Pushing sixty now, Woodson was still the only person Russell seemed to respect and defer to, and Billy would touch base with him from time to time, just to get insight into his client's erratic personality.

"It takes some time to gain his trust," Woodson had told him early on, "but I've always thought kids like Russell were worth the effort. They don't have many people who really care about them."

Woodson had shepherded the young basketball star through his personal minefields, and he believed Russell's skills were formidable enough to earn him a ticket out of the projects. He was right. Unfortunately, that ride began at an obscure junior college in Mississippi, of all places.

The major-college recruiters had been scared off by the kid's academic problems and rumors that he enjoyed hanging out with gangbangers. Still, if a player had enough talent, there were schools that would give him a chance. Southwest Mississippi State was one such institution, always willing to gamble on risky prospects.

Another coaching friend had told Billy to keep an eye on Russell, that the long, lean forward had the physical tools to play in the NBA. And maybe, just maybe, he had the game to develop into a solid pro. Over time he had become much more than that. He was an all-star on the verge of becoming a very rich young man.

The agent had also been warned: Russell was carrying some serious emotional baggage. That did not particularly trouble Billy, who was supremely confident in his influence over clients and his powers of persuasion. He believed most anyone could be rehabilitated, steered in the right direction, in the proper environment. It was up to him to create that environment.

Billy got to know Russell on his occasional trips through Mississippi. According to the player's junior-college coach, no other reputable agents appeared to be interested, so the door was wide open. "Good luck getting him to listen," the coach said.

Billy not only got in Russell's ear, he eventually signed him and then arranged for a tryout in Orlando as an undrafted free agent. Slowly but surely, Russell established himself as the centerpiece of a team that was beginning to emerge in the Eastern Conference. It was increasingly apparent that there weren't many guys in the league like him. And he was a financial bargain for the franchise.

Now, near the end of his third season, it seemed there was little standing in the way of that huge contract. Russell had paid his dues. He was a proven commodity and expected to be treated like one.

"What time is your shootaround?" Billy said, breaking the silence.

"One. Can you drop me at the arena? I got somebody coming to pick me up later."

"Sure. So we've got time to sit and discuss this? That's why I'm here."

Russell took a big swallow of his Coke and rubbed his eyes. He nodded Billy down the hallway toward the game room.

"Let's talk in here," he said. "We can play a game of Destiny, too. I'll crush you."

"Destiny? I'm not familiar with that one."

"We're shooters, defenders of Earth's last safe city."

"Seems like a lot to tackle this morning," Billy said. "First things first. We'll talk and then we'll shoot."

CHAPTER EIGHT

The men parted company near the players' entrance to the Amway Center, and Billy circled around to the executive suites. The agent caught a glimpse of Lawrence West, the Orlando Magic's general manager, sitting in his office. West waved him in.

"Seems like I've been seeing more of you here recently," he said, rising to shake hands. "Wonder why that is?"

Billy laughed and took a seat.

The men had a good relationship, considering the adversarial nature of their professions. West was new on the job in Orlando when Billy convinced him to take a chance on Russell, the undrafted rookie. It proved to be one of the best moves either had ever made. West had shrewdly built a contending team in the three years since, while Billy's profile had been raised as Russell blossomed into a star attraction.

"I hope you'll be seeing even more of me," Billy said. "We're coming down the home stretch, here."

"Let's don't jump too far ahead of ourselves. We're in the playoff picture with less than two weeks to go. Not many people were predicting that at the start of the season."

"A masterful job by the GM, I must say. Magical almost. I must also say that Russell Mann is a hell of a talent to build around."

"Agreed. Who knew at the time? I remember you almost begging me to give the guy a tryout. I guess we both got a little lucky."

"Agreed."

West grinned and circled around his desk to close the office door. "Billy, I think we can also agree that your client likes it here in sunny Florida," he said. "Likes it a lot, in fact."

"What's not to like? This is a place where anything you can dream is possible. The Disney theory. Of course, Russell is going to have a lot of options after the season. There's plenty of interest already. The way the cap is increasing, a forward with his skills may be worth a hundred million dollars."

"A hundred million? C'mon. Isn't it scary for an agent like you to even say that number out loud, with a straight face? You don't believe that. A hundred million dollars for an undrafted free agent?"

"It's a great American story. Again, anything is possible in this brave, new NBA world, and we'll see soon enough. In the meantime, good luck to you and your team. I don't want to take up any more of your time today. This is just a courtesy call."

"I appreciate that. And let me return the favor. This is just you and me talking, nothing official."

"Certainly."

"The ownership group here would like to re-sign your client to a long-term deal. He's earned it. But I must say that we're still a little concerned."

"About?"

"About Russell's … demeanor. I think our P.R. department has made strides on that front. He's a lot more popular with the fans — winning tends to have that effect on people — but he's still prickly, doesn't smile much. He's never going to be an engaging sort of guy, never going to lead the league in endorsements or be an ideal face of the franchise. I'm sure you realize that."

"None of us ever thought he was the second coming of Magic Johnson. He's just a pit bull of a small forward. Long and tough and skilled. He's turned out to be a better player than either of us could have predicted, an exceptional value for your organization. And he's only twenty-five and getting better. That's why I'm sitting here right now with a smile on my face."

"And that's great, obviously. The real concern is off the court, the company he keeps and that sort of thing. We just don't need any kind of legal troubles. Ownership wants to be absolutely sure before it invests more millions in your pit bull — not a hundred million but many millions."

Billy furrowed his brow. "He's already been here three years, so you should have a pretty good idea of what you've got. Considering his background, I think he's done well. This is a kid that came from a really bad home situation, like a lot of others in this league, and he's turned himself into an all-star player. But you can't wipe away the past entirely."

"The question," West said, "is whether he's learned from it. Is he *maturing*? Can he be a team leader for the duration of his contract? At that salary, he has to be somebody the other guys will look up to and follow. He has to stay out of trouble. He has to be a real star, across the board."

"You're not telling me something here, Larry. What is it?"

West hesitated. "Again, this is just between us."

"Of course."

"I'm a little concerned about an incident in Orlando several days ago. A guy that Russell knew from back in New York, kind of a shady character with a rap sheet, was out late after one of our games and ended up getting shot. They found him face down in a ditch out on the edge of town."

"Murdered?"

"Shot in the back of the head. It's still an open case. Russell had given this guy a ticket to the game, and they apparently had a drink or two afterwards at a club over in Park-Highland, then went their separate ways. A few hours later he turned up dead. I'm not accusing anybody of anything, but it's worrisome. I keep hearing little things about it."

"Why didn't *I* hear anything about it?"

"I can't answer that. Your client apparently didn't see a need to tell you."

"Did you talk to Russell?"

"Of course, after the cops interviewed him. There was no connection they could find, so it passed with very little notice. The guy — his name was Blue something — had a lot to drink and apparently got with the wrong people in the middle of the night. It happens."

"Without knowing more, I'd have to say that your concerns about Russell are a bit misplaced. A whole bunch of players in the league come from violent backgrounds. How many of them do you know that go around shooting old friends in the middle of the night?"

"Not many, and again, I'm not accusing anybody. If I thought Russell was involved in any way, we'd be finished with him in a heartbeat. I just know that he'd really been laying low for most of the season, focusing on the job at hand — a serious pro. He wasn't even going out after the games. I get a sense that something has changed. He's been playing great, but there have been more odd characters hanging around. There's a little different vibe."

"If it makes you feel better, Larry, I'll redouble my efforts to stay in closer contact with him. This is a delicate time for all of us, and I want to do everything to guarantee his success. That should never be in question with any of my clients."

"I trust you," West said, "but sometimes an agent can only do so much. We both know that."

The men stood and shook hands. "Good luck to the Magic," Billy said. He walked out of the office suddenly wondering if Russell might be better off playing somewhere else, starting fresh. There soon would be other offers on the table.

CHAPTER NINE

The woman stopped at the end of the driveway, removed her sunglasses and stared at the gray contemporary on the hill. *Silver Oak.* She had come up with the name herself.

The drive used to be a reflex action — leave the office, drop the top on her convertible, soak up the sun as she headed out of town. She always enjoyed pushing her Mercedes at the end, through the twisting turns toward the Tennessee River. Toward their home.

Rocky Top Estates was a rich enclave, a side of Knoxville that few of its citizens would ever know. After all these months, maybe she didn't know it so well either.

Finally, she eased up the driveway and parked in front of the garage. She could see the tranquil river flowing in the distance. The dock, the houseboat. The scene of the crime.

The last time she was at the house, after the kidnapping, she loaded up her car with a few belongings and left. It was supposed to be just a break, a trip home to clear her head. She knew she'd miss Billy before long; she always did. She'd be back.

But she never returned.

Rachel reached into her jeans pocket and pulled out the key ring. The locks and security code had been changed, but she was prepared. She walked to the front porch, slid in the key, and turned the knob. Once inside she disabled the alarm and stopped to look around. She was excited, but her breathing was calm and steady.

The house still felt captivating with its stunning views, vaulted ceilings, and exotic oak floors and trim. It had been remodeled before they moved in and was loaded with furnishings that she had found at markets around Charleston. The place had *personality*. Too bad it had become notorious.

She walked to the window and gazed out at the water. She loved the water.

If not for her father, they would never have gotten the property. Bradley King was a rabid sports fan and clicked with Billy from the start. When the couple moved from Atlanta, he made sure the agent got off to a good start with his new business, and that Rachel was comfortable.

And she had indeed been comfortable, more comfortable than restless for the first time in her life. Great memories were made here. Lasting memories.

She stopped in the living room and frowned. There used to be pictures hanging on the wall — her and Billy, posing with clients, relaxing on the river with friends, tailgating at Neyland Stadium, partying at all sorts of sports events. The pictures were gone now, the wall space bare.

Rachel resisted pouring herself a drink at the bar. The bottle of Blanton's single barrel bourbon, her favorite, was still right there on the shelf. Too early. She turned and walked slowly up the stairs to the master suite.

There was the bed where they once made love so passionately. They were good together. Chemistry. She smiled until she noticed the picture on the dresser. Billy was standing with a tall blonde, his arm around her waist. They both looked happy. Too happy.

She opened the closet door and turned on the light. The picture frames from downstairs had been stacked in a corner. There she was on top, smoking hot in that red bikini. Just above, hanging on the rod, were what remained of the clothes she hadn't taken when she left. Even the black leather outfit with the whip she had worn as a Valentine's Day gift to Billy.

No, he hadn't completely rid himself of her. He couldn't. She would give him plenty more to think about.

On her way out of the bedroom, another picture stopped Rachel in her tracks. *John Beckett.* One arm around her shoulder, the other resting on his brother's shoulder. The three of them, standing tall. Smiles all around.

Rachel stared at the image. *What would John say now to her now? What would Billy say?* She couldn't help herself. She lifted the frame from its place on the wall and tucked it under her arm as she walked back down the steps.

It's Not Over Yet. Not by a long shot.

CHAPTER TEN

The Knicks were no match for the Magic. Russell Mann was making sure of that.

Orlando had built a twenty-point lead by halftime, and its best player, apparently energized for the battle with his hometown team, had already tallied twenty-two points and ten rebounds by himself.

The Magic were back on the floor, and Russell was casually flipping jump shots as the players warmed up for the second half. He grinned and winked at Billy and Holly Grace, who were stretching their legs across the way in front of their half-court seats. Maybe he was just winking at *her.*

Holly was an LPGA touring pro who had driven up from her home in Fort Lauderdale. Tall and blonde, with a dazzling smile, she never failed to turn heads. She obviously was the focus of her agent's attention at the moment.

"Russell is making this look easy," she said. "I didn't realize he was *this* good. Guess you have to get close to really appreciate it."

Billy nodded with authority. "Kind of like golf, right? The Knicks are helping the cause a little. They're bad. But yeah, he's really good. He might just carry this bunch to the playoffs."

The horn sounded and the fans began to settle back into their seats. The team's rising stature was evident in the stands of the Amway Center. For the first time since the days of Shaquille O'Neal and Penny Hardaway, Magic games were a hot ticket in town. Tonight the place was packed.

"Looks like the Orlando boys are a lot better than your Heat this season," Billy said. "That's a new twist in the Sunshine State."

"*My* Heat? I may be a South Florida transplant — one of millions — but I'm still an Atlanta girl at heart. Go Hawks."

"Now *there's* a winner. Are they still in the league?"

She smirked in that sexy sort of way and tapped him on the arm.

Holly lived at the Breakers Club of Fort Lauderdale, where she owned a condo along a picturesque fairway of the club's championship golf course. She had become something of a celebrity after winning her first LPGA tournament the previous summer.

With the tour schedule showing an open date this week, Holly decided to make the three-hour drive up to Orlando and spend some time with her agent. Mix a little business and pleasure, not necessarily in that order.

Their connection had been getting tighter since she joined Billy on a trip to Las Vegas a few months earlier. They had watched in awe as another of his clients, Cassie Haynes, a mixed martial arts fighter from Tennessee, won a world championship with a stunning knockout of the alleged "baddest woman on the planet."

Their time together had left an enduring impression.

"I still find myself thinking about that night — that whole trip, really," Holly said earlier on the way to the arena. "I'll just be walking along somewhere and a smile comes over my face. How is Cassie anyway?"

"She's doing great. Getting her and her brother set up out there, away from the craziness of their family, has really helped. She's like a new person."

"I have a hard time envisioning the two of them living in Las Vegas."

"It's a little different than Newport, Tennessee, for sure. But Cassie and Thomas have a daily routine that doesn't change much. They don't lose focus, and they're working hard. She's going to be fighting again soon."

"What about their grandfather? I really liked him. Hated to hear what happened."

"Yeah, Sheriff is going to be in prison for a while. I talk to him every now and then. He was up to his eyeballs in all sorts of unlawful activity, and it was just a matter of time before it caught up to him. I hate it, too."

"Unlawful activity? Is that what they call solicitation of murder, cocaine trafficking, and moonshining up in those Tennessee mountains?"

"Where Sheriff comes from, that's called business as usual."

Out on the court, the Knicks had whittled six points off the Orlando lead. Russell strolled from the Magic's bench to the scorer's table and knelt, waiting for a stoppage of play to get back in the game. Finally, the ball went out of bounds and the horn sounded.

He ripped off his warm-ups and walked with his ever-present scowl over to the man he would be guarding. He was a notorious beast in the weight room, and it showed. His body had matured into a ripped two hundred and forty pounds, though he still moved like a much smaller man.

Even with a sizeable lead, there would be no letup in his approach to the game. Not against the Knicks.

The first time he touched the ball, Russell threaded a no-look pass inside to center Jermaine Nickels for an easy score. Next time down the court, he took the ball at the top of the key and dribbled left through traffic for a short pull-up jumper, his signature shot. The Knicks quickly inbounded the ball and pushed it toward the other end, but even in retreat Russell's long arms and quick hands seemed to cover every angle. He stole a pass and dribbled the other way for an emphatic dunk.

Timeout, Knicks.

It was the kind of frenetic sequence that set Russell apart from other NBA forwards, and it turned the tide back in Orlando's favor for good. The fans rose from their seats with another chorus of "Suuuper Mann" as Russell's jubilant teammates spilled onto the court to escort him to the bench. Holly and Billy looked at each other with eyebrows raised. The flurry had left them as impressed as anybody.

"Nice client you've got there," Holly said.

"What can I say? Our company has a deep and talented roster."

"I've never had a chance to meet Russell. Is he as intimidating as he looks?"

"He's just a New Yorker who's all about basketball. Not a bad guy, just a little rough around the edges. You'll get a chance to meet him later at this club down the street. He wanted us to drop by and have a drink with him."

"Why hasn't he ever come to any of the BBE get-togethers?"

"He's not the most social client we've got, kind of a loner. We invite him but he always seems to have a reason not to come. It's just as well."

The Magic kept up their assault and held a thirty-point lead early in the fourth quarter when coach Jeff Sanders began to pull his starters. Russell went to the bench with thirty-six points, hailed by yet another standing ovation.

Billy smiled to himself. He noticed that his pulse had quickened. It was going to be a very productive offseason indeed.

CHAPTER ELEVEN

Hocus Pocus was a popular place for Magic fans on game nights. Russell was already at the club in the Milk District, surrounded by friends and well-wishers, when Billy and Holly walked in. They had stopped at the hotel to make a few phone calls. The agent could easily field a dozen concerns from clients in a day.

The raucous bar scene caught Billy a bit off guard. Russell was beaming as he towered over the crowd. He threw back the last of one drink and was quickly handed another. The star was basking in his glory, at the expense of the poor Knicks. Clearly, he was beginning to relish the superstar treatment.

"I thought you said he was anti-social," Holly said as she slid into a booth across from Billy.

"Usually is. Looks happier than I've seen him in a while. Almost giddy. I don't think he's used to having people pay so much attention to him. Orlando hasn't exactly been a basketball hotbed, and Russell tends to be pretty aloof."

"He did play a great game tonight. He deserves to have some fun."

Billy nodded and looked around the place. The bar area, with its huge saltwater aquariums as backdrops, was packed three deep. A throng of young women bathed in colored lights on the dance floor, gyrating to a heavy Latin beat. Another sultry night in Florida was in full swing.

Russell had an entourage with him, three rough characters that kept a close watch on the gathering. Clubs of all stripes in the city had been tense in the wake of recent shootings, and these men looked like bodyguards. Billy wasn't sure. He thought he could see the bulge of a firearm inside one man's jacket, and that was troubling.

A waitress dropped off a couple of frosty pale ales at the table. After a few minutes, Russell noticed Billy and broke free from his admirers. He folded his long frame into the booth beside Holly.

"Russell Mann," he said, extending a hand. "And let me guess, you're Holly Grace. The golfer. Billy said you were coming."

She smiled and shook his hand. "Nice to meet you, Russell. Great game tonight. You guys are on a roll."

Russell held her hand and gazed for a few seconds, admiringly. He apparently was feeling no pain and didn't mind testing his appeal.

"Why don't you come and play golf at my course," he said. "You can give me some lessons."

"That would be interesting, I'm sure. I haven't seen many six-eight guys out on the course lately. Have you been playing long?"

Russell looked at Billy and laughed. "Hell, I don't even have clubs, but I'd be happy to buy some if you'd come out. I'm a quick learner. Ask our agent here, he'll tell you."

"I'm sure you are. I appreciate the offer, but I'm just in town for the evening. Back to work tomorrow."

"Where do you live?" he said, leaning in closer.

"Fort Lauderdale," she said, and began fidgeting with her purse. "Can you let me out for a minute, Russell? I need to visit the ladies room."

She scooted out and walked past his leering companions, who were never far from earshot. Russell sat back down in front of Billy.

"I like Holly," he said, admiring her backside. "She's fine."

"Easy there, big man," Billy said. "You need to chill. It's getting late."

"Everybody wants me to chill. We're off tomorrow, so no need to worry. I can sleep as late as I want."

"By the way, who are these guys hanging out here with you? I don't remember seeing them before."

"Just some friends. Two from Hunts Point and a guy who lives down here. The short one is Tariq; I call him T-Bone. He's my man. He watches after me."

Billy glanced over and could see all three of them sizing him up. "They're not carrying guns in here, are they?" he said.

"Maybe. I don't know. People need protection. There's a lot of dangerous things going on."

"So I hear. Why didn't you tell me about your friend who was murdered here a few days ago?"

"Nothing to say. I didn't have anything to do with that; hadn't seen the dude in years. He just called me up and wanted a ticket. I took care of him, and we had a drink after the game. That was it."

"That wasn't it for him. Somebody killed him. I was looking back at the newspaper story online earlier today. The cops said he was shot in the back of the head, execution style."

"I told them all I knew, which wasn't much. I was at home asleep at the time. I was as surprised as anybody when I heard what happened the next morning. Why are you asking me about it now?"

"Russell, we've talked about this before. You need to lay low, mind your business. It's my job to keep things on track. The season is about over and you've got a lot on the line. Any kind of trouble could cost you big-time, especially with the Magic."

"And cost *you*."

Billy seemed startled. His voice rose against the music.

"This isn't about me. People are watching *you*, and they're all making judgments, on and off the court. I thought you had been keeping to yourself late at night, playing video games or whatever. Trouble is easy to find in the bars, especially for high-profile athletes."

"I been cool, but I was getting tired of sitting at the house. We're winning and the fans are juiced up. It's springtime in Florida, man. I hope you and Miss Holly are enjoying yourselves this evening. Order more drinks, some food. It's my treat."

"We appreciate that, but it's getting near midnight and we're gonna head on. I just wanted to introduce Holly, since we're all on the same team. I'm glad you and I had a chance to talk this morning. There'll be plenty more to discuss in the coming weeks. You just stay focused, keep playing like you have been, and with a little luck we'll see the Magic in the playoffs. Russell Mann will be a hero in this town."

"I like the sound of that."

Both men were standing beside the booth when Holly returned. Russell walked over to T-Bone and whispered something in his ear. T-Bone then left the room, and his companions followed.

"Tell you what," Russell said to Billy. "If it makes you feel better, I'll walk out with you."

He handed the waitress some cash and they headed toward the exit together. Outside the club, an older model black sedan with eye-catching gold wheels pulled up to the curb. Billy could see T-Bone behind the wheel and flashed a disapproving glance at Russell.

"Don't worry," the big man said. "He's just giving me a lift home. I'll be in bed before you are."

They shook hands, and Russell nodded toward Holly.

"Really nice to meet you," he said. "Hope it's not the last time."

CHAPTER TWELVE

Russell didn't go home. He and his cronies were headed to a place they called the Flophouse. It was a secluded bungalow in Orlovista where the gang congregated regularly to party.

There were always plenty of diversions — cocaine, expensive liquors, sometimes a little female affection for rent. Tonight it was just the four men.

T-Bone opened the side door and flipped on the lights. He looked after the place, spent most nights in a back bedroom. A diminutive man with a boyish face, he had grown up in the Bronx with Russell and welcomed the chance to come down to Florida and be of service to his friend. They shared the same hardened outlook on life, the suspicion of most everyone around them, a willingness to take matters into their own hands. The player had grown used to having him nearby.

"Home, sweet home," T-Bone said, pulling a round of beers from the refrigerator. "We should have brought your agent along. Or his blond friend."

"How 'bout that Holly?" Russell said. "Don't know if she's great at golf — I mean, she's a pro — but she's definitely the finest golfer I've ever seen up close. I think the agent would agree. Billy enjoyed having her right there beside him, didn't he?"

"Up until the end there at the club," T-Bone said. "Did you see the look on his face once she left and it was just you two in the booth? Dude wasn't happy."

Russell laughed. "He thought you boys looked scary and was asking me about guns. What Billy don't know won't hurt him. He just needs to stick to his job — making me richer than rich for the long haul. He's smart."

"He's motivated, too. Right?"

"I'm going to make him more money over the next few years than a boatload of his other clients. Some of those NFL brothers are killing themselves for nothing. In three or four years they'll never even know they were in the league, and they won't hardly be able to walk. I'll still be pounding the rock in ten years, making serious bank."

Russell laughed and walked down the hall to a wall safe. He quickly spun through the combination. "Turn on some tunes, T-Bone," he yelled back. The safe door opened, and he pulled out a baggie with white powder about a finger deep.

Cocaine never used to appeal to Russell — he came from a different drug culture — but it was starting to grow on him. A quick pick-me-up that didn't linger in the blood had special value. Easy to see how some athletes got hooked on the stuff.

Russell plopped down at the kitchen table and unfurled the baggie. He dipped in a knife blade and raked out five hefty lines on the glass — two for him and one for each of his cohorts. His eyes lit up as he snorted the first one.

"How 'bout those Knicks, Kimbo?" he said, passing a glass straw to his barrel-chested friend from the Bronx. "We ripped their hearts out. Felt good."

Kimbo inhaled his line with vigor and laid his head back. There was a long, slow exhale.

"They ain't been worth nothing long as I remember," he said. "Don't guess you'll be coming back to the city and playing for those dogs."

"No way."

"Where, then?"

"Billy thinks staying in Orlando makes the most sense. But it's up to me. I like it here … the weather and the women are gold. And there's always Disney World."

The men laughed and kept getting higher and talking crazier, like old times. In fact, Russell hadn't changed much at all. He just had an endless supply of cash now to fuel his ego and off-the-court interests.

"You better start dialing it down, bro," Kimbo said. "That's what your boy Billy was saying, right? You need to stay outta trouble. Sounded like your daddy."

Russell's face tightened. "What daddy?"

"Didn't mean anything, bro. Just never used to hear that when we were scrapin' round the hood."

"He didn't have nothing to lose then," the third man said. "Now look. Big star, playing on TV every night, buying drinks for people he don't know, throwing down the blow. Definitely not scrapin' round no more."

"Super Mann," T-Bone said. "Big S on his chest. That's right."

"Don't you boys forget it either," Russell said, checking his watch. The morning was moving toward one thirty. "I think I've had enough. Take me on to the house."

T-Bone glanced over at Kimbo with a coy smile. "So you don't want to go by and see Angel first, Russell? I'm sure she's up."

"Shit, that's back in Parramore. No sense running around down there this time of night. People get crazy."

"You remember Angel, don't you? Best rub ever, isn't that what you said? Angel dust is what you called her. Wild child. All I gotta do is call and she'll be waiting."

Russell hesitated. He'd had just one encounter with the buxom Puerto Rican, and it was memorable indeed. Her heart, and everything else, was in the right place.

"I don't know, bruh," he said. "Been a long night."

"You already got a good feel going. Get you one more little whiff and let's go. We'll find something to get into while you and Angel get to know each other better. You said you could sleep late, anyway."

Russell stroked his chin for a moment and then picked up the knife. He grinned as he dipped it back into the baggie. One more line for the road.

CHAPTER THIRTEEN

Billy rolled over in bed and was face-to-face with her again. Holly smiled and ran her hand softly along his cheek. What a reminder: She was gorgeous at any hour of the day.

"Good morning," she said.

"Good morning to you. Sleep well?"

"I did, but I need to get up and moving. I'm supposed to meet my swing coach at the club about two o'clock. Time to get back on the highway."

"Don't go yet." Billy pulled her closer. He had almost forgotten what it was like to have her beside him, to hold her in his arms, caress that magnificent body. And to think he had once resisted the idea of making love to her.

"Encore?" he said.

She reached down and gave his butt a quick pat as she rolled out of bed. "Sorry. Next time."

The encounter had been earthmoving, as always, but where their personal relationship stood wasn't exactly clear. Billy had helped guide Holly from obscurity to the winner's circle on the LPGA tour. He brought out the best in her professionally, gave her confidence and helped craft her vivacious image. But the lines were getting blurry.

At the end of the Las Vegas trip, perhaps lightheaded from it all, Holly had blurted out that she might be falling in love with him. Months later, neither of them could be sure. Little more had been said.

The attraction was probably more a mix of lust and loneliness than love. Their hectic schedules kept them on the road a good bit of the time, so it was hard to get close to people. Billy kept thinking that any self-respecting agent should keep his hands off the clients. Besides, he was still torn by the whole split with Rachel. The disillusionment was fresh in his mind again.

Holly ducked into the bathroom and turned on the shower. Twenty minutes later the door opened and she emerged, looking like a magazine cover — the tan, finely tuned athlete, resplendent in her white capri pants and coral top. She reminded him of … Rachel.

"You look like a *player*," Billy said admiringly, still stretched out on the bed with his phone in hand. "Not just another pretty face. That's for damn sure."

"It's time to start seeing that face on the leader board again. I need to get back to work."

The early part of the golf season had been a mixed bag for Holly. After winning her first LPGA tournament last summer, and finishing in the top twenty on the money list, she was becoming a familiar name on tour. Billy had negotiated a couple of national ad campaigns and other endorsements over the winter, taking advantage of her marketing appeal. But the success hadn't carried over to the golf course in the spring like both had expected. Holly was pressing again, thinking too much the way golfers tend to do. That had been an issue in previous years.

She sat on the edge of the bed and rubbed his shoulders.

"Where do things stand with us, really?" she said. "Seems like we've been avoiding the conversation."

Billy took a deep swallow. "What do you mean?"

"You remember what I told you at the Atlanta airport that day? I've regretted saying it out loud like that. And then, other days I don't. I really do think I love you. There — I said it again."

"What about today?"

"I don't know."

From the beginning, Billy had feared that getting too deeply involved with her would be self-defeating for them both. Holly's slow start to the season had magnified those fears. Now they seemed to be in limbo. Billy either needed to pull back or fully invest, and investing emotionally in women had never been easy for him.

He flipped his phone on the bedspread and looked deeply into her eyes.

"I honestly don't know what to say. You're a woman that deserves the best. I'm not sure I would qualify."

She flashed that seductive smile. "Don't sell yourself short. We both know that's not the case." Billy blushed a bit and pulled up the sheet.

"I know you've been hurt before," Holly said. "The thing that happened with Rachel … I didn't know her, but it doesn't matter. It's over, right?"

"It's over for *me*."

"What does *that* mean?"

Billy felt compelled to tell her the whole story as she sat on the bed beside him. How Rachel had disappeared.

The messages, the implications. The recent trip to New Orleans with her father. How it might not be over for *her*.

"So she's been *stalking* you?" Holly said. "Seriously?"

"I don't know for sure. There's something going on. Until I figure out what, it may not be a good idea for you and me to be too involved beyond our business relationship. We probably shouldn't be together like this."

Holly walked to the sliding glass door and gazed across at the busy runways of Orlando International Airport. The Hyatt Regency in the terminal building there had always been one of Billy's favorite hotels, a unique blend of adventure and convenience.

There was a puff of smoke in the distance as another commercial airliner touched down on the pavement.

"What does she look like?"

The question caught Billy off guard. *What does she look like?*

"Rachel. You have a picture?"

Billy reluctantly picked up his phone and scrolled through the images. He finally tapped one and turned the screen toward Holly.

"There she is. Rachel King, in better times."

Holly took the phone and studied the statuesque woman posing on the sundeck of Billy's houseboat in a royal blue, one-piece swimsuit. She looked like a model.

"I think I've seen this woman," Holly said, narrowing her eyes. "I think I've *met* this woman."

Billy sat up in bed. "Seriously? Where?"

"At a tournament a few weeks ago, out in Phoenix. She came up to me as I was walking off the practice green. Said something like, 'Better be careful.' I didn't know what she was talking about, and it kind of startled me, but no big deal. People are always saying crazy stuff. I didn't see her again."

"Are you sure?"

Holly looked at the picture again. "She was wearing big sunglasses, but I'm pretty sure. She's very attractive. Does this mean she's stalking me, too?"

"I would hope not. I'd be willing to bet it was someone else."

"Maybe."

She handed his phone back, and Billy rolled out of bed.

"We still need to talk," Holly said. "I'm serious. When will I see you again?"

"Soon. I want us to stay in close touch, regardless. Let me know if you see or hear anything about Rachel. I don't think there's anything for you to worry about. I just want to be sure."

She nodded and slung her travel bag over her shoulder. "Now that you've scared me, I have to go."

"Wait," he said. "Let me throw on some clothes real quick and I'll walk you to your car."

Rachel was on both of their minds as they stepped into the glass elevator, which looked down on the bustling airport concourse. Travelers were moving in all directions. The couple threaded their way through the Hyatt lobby and out to valet parking.

A young attendant took the ticket and sprinted around the corner of the garage. Within a minute, he was pulling up in Holly's white Audi convertible. Billy walked with her to the driver's door and gave her an affectionate kiss and hug.

"Be careful," he said as she slid behind the wheel.

"*You* be careful," she responded. "What time is your flight, anyway?"

"I've got a couple of hours. I just have to take the elevator down and walk right into the security line. I'll arrive in Knoxville not long after you pull into Fort Lauderdale. We'll talk again soon. In the meantime, hit 'em sweet."

The car door closed and Holly dropped the top of her convertible. She pulled her long hair back with an elastic band and donned a pair of dark Maui Jim sunglasses. *What a woman.* One last, longing smile and she pulled away.

Billy turned and walked back toward the lobby. The news on the radio was blaring as he passed the valet stand. There had been a shooting in downtown Orlando early that morning. Two men killed. No suspects in custody.

Police were looking for a black sedan.

CHAPTER FOURTEEN

gent Orange hadn't gotten much use lately, and today was a perfect day to air her out. Sunny and warm. A gentle breeze blowing across the Tennessee River late in the afternoon.

Billy was cleaning the glass in the boat's cabin when he heard his name called. He stepped onto the deck and looked up at the house. Claire was standing on the veranda.

"C'mon down," he yelled. Billy couldn't help but notice the bounce in her step as she made her way along the pathway. Finally, she eased onto the dock and over to the railing of the white boat.

"How long have you been back?" she said.

"Not long. I just felt like taking a little cruise. It's been a while. Want to ride along?"

"That's a hard offer to refuse, Mr. Beckett. I could use some fresh air myself. How's Russell, anyway?"

"He's good, played a great game last night. I think we're right on track with the new contract, if we can just keep him on the straight and narrow. I wouldn't call it a slam dunk, but everything is shaping up."

"He has every reason to behave himself."

"Yes, but … it is Russell we're talking about. I always get the feeling he's in the danger zone, one way or another."

"And Holly?" Claire said with a slight snicker.

"She's great."

"Of course."

"Anything new and exciting here?"

"As a matter of fact, there is. That's why I stopped by."

"I'd love to hear it. I just need to get some stuff from the house, and then we'll head out. You game for that?"

"Absolutely."

There was a dreamy smile on Claire's face that seemed to be lingering. Billy stopped and cocked his head. He looked at her curiously.

"What?" she said.

"Sit down here. I know when you're anxious to tell me something, so go ahead. Let's talk."

"All right. Remember, I said I knew where to start if we decided to get into the music business."

"If," Billy said, raising an index finger for emphasis.

She nodded. "Well, I have an old friend from Belle Meade. Her name is Michelle, and she has a brother named Tyler. He's a lot younger than us; I guess he may have been a surprise to their parents. I spent a lot of time at their house growing up, and he was always fooling around with guitars and other instruments. All sorts of instruments. He was kind of a skinny, nerdy kid back then. A loner really, but a music prodigy. He could play by ear or read sheet music and play anything thrown at him by the time he was a teenager."

Claire tapped at her cell phone a few times. "Well, look at him now."

She turned the screen toward Billy. There was a young man with toned biceps in a black t-shirt and jeans, holding a guitar by the neck, upside down with the body braced against his side.

Billy took the phone in his hand for a closer look. The long, wavy hair, the confident smile, the rugged good looks. Could be a country music star's poster, an ad for Taylor guitars, maybe an album cover.

"I'm afraid to know where you're headed with this, Claire."

"This is *him*. He goes by Ty now. Ty Nelson. He's one of the hottest young talents in Nashville — amazing songwriter and guitarist, with a voice to match. He's our newest client."

Billy frowned. "I didn't think we'd made any decisions on that yet."

"I had to commit, under the circumstances."

"What circumstances?"

"Have you seen The Songmasters on television? It's a national competition that plays out in Los Angeles; you've probably seen some snippets."

"Maybe. I can't keep up with all the talent shows."

"Well, Ty is one of the final ten this season; he's going to be a major star in the music world."

"You're sure of that?"

"Yes, I am. Michelle, his sister, was telling me about this competition a few weeks ago and we got to talking. Ty had been looking for a new agent before any of this came down. Now his phone is ringing constantly."

"And you think he's going to sign a management contract with little ol' Claire from the neighborhood? Because why?"

"Because I'm a damn good advocate. And he was always a little smitten with me, if I do say so myself. I've stayed in contact with the family through the years. We're still close. They trust me."

Billy got up and started walking aimlessly around the boat.

"What was it I was looking for? Oh yeah, the broom. Or was it the anchor to tie around my neck?"

Claire grabbed his arm. "C'mon, Billy. The timing on this couldn't be better for us. Are we in or out? Tell me now."

"So our entertainment division," he said, using air quotes, "has one client, maybe. Then what?"

"We'll see. If Ty's career takes off like I think it will, we'll have more people — good people — wanting to jump on board than you can imagine. That's a boat analogy, by the way. It's going to happen fast."

"And that worries me, too."

"You let me worry about it and just keep doing your thing. You're so skilled at handling the athletes; they love working with you and Jackson. I've already done a lot of research on the entertainment side, been talking to my attorney friend in Nashville. I'll lay it all out there with some numbers and projections in a formal presentation, like I said. This just couldn't wait."

"You've given this a lot of thought."

"To be honest, it's been on my mind since the first day I got involved with your company. It just makes perfect sense."

Billy stared out at the river. He wasn't convinced yet and needed to clear his head. A lot of decisions, good decisions, had been made on that boat.

"I'll think about it. Let me run up to the house, and then we'll go."

"One more thing," Claire said. "Ty has invited us to come down to Nashville on Friday night. They're throwing kind of a private party at the Bluebird Café as a sendoff for The Songmasters, and he's going to play a few tunes. He wants to meet you. We can take Jackson along, too. It'll be fun."

Billy let out a deep sigh. Finally, he shook his head and smiled.

"Premier," he said.

"What?"

"The new name. Premier Sports and Entertainment. PSE."

Claire chuckled. "So you've been thinking about that, huh?"

"A little."

"I like it. Why don't we just celebrate a fresh start, right here and now. I've got a really good bottle of Cabernet in the car, and you've got the boat. Sounds like a party."

"So you brought celebratory wine? That was presumptuous."

She walked over and gave him a big hug. "Yes it was. Let's go."

CHAPTER FIFTEEN

The banging on the door shook Billy from his stupor. He could hear it all the way from his bedroom upstairs.

His head was throbbing, a painful reminder that it was never a good idea to mix red wine and Heineken. He rubbed his eyes and craned his neck toward the clock on the dresser. Seven twenty. *Seven twenty!*

"All right, all right," Billy muttered to himself as he crawled out of bed and threw on a t-shirt and sweatpants. He staggered down the steps and over to the front door. Through the peephole, he could see the man's face glaring at him.

The door opened and James Bosken burst into the foyer, brushing Billy's shoulder as he passed.

"James?" Billy said groggily. "What's wrong?"

"I'll tell you what's wrong. She left."

Billy's eyes narrowed. "Who left where?"

"Claire. Is she here?"

"No. It's not even seven thirty. Why *would* she be?"

"She was here last night, right?" Bosken hissed.

"Right. So…"

"Well, she came home half drunk — more than half — and started carrying on about her big plans. With *you*. It didn't take long to hear about the two of you riding around on the river, sipping wine and having a grand old time. I didn't care for it. Things kind of went south from there."

"How far south?"

"Pretty far."

Bosken looked up at Billy with contempt. He was a sturdy man, but a few inches shorter and several pounds lighter. He always seemed to have his emotions in check, buttoned down. It was expected from one of Knoxville's most celebrated defense attorneys.

Not now. Bosken was fuming.

Billy scratched the stubble on his cheek and tried to blink away the fog as he turned toward the kitchen. He was hoping to defuse the situation, once he figured out exactly what the situation was.

"How about some coffee, James?"

"I'm not here for coffee."

"What exactly are you here for then? It's a little early for anything else."

"I'm looking for Claire. She walked out and didn't come back. You know the last thing she said? Maybe we should just split up, go our separate ways. I've heard her say all kinds of nutty things through the years, but never that."

"She's never told me she was thinking that way. I certainly didn't hear it last night. She was in a good mood, excited."

"I'll bet she was."

"You're reading too much into this," Billy said. "We were just celebrating some changes with the business. They were her ideas, and I finally agreed. We went out on the boat, then came back here and sat outside by the fire pit a while. She left well before midnight."

"That's it?"

"We're just friends, James. New partners and old friends. Nothing more or less."

Bosken looked suspiciously at the agent, who had a well-deserved reputation as a smooth talker. He was having none of it.

"I think there's more."

"Why do you say that?"

"It's becoming more obvious. You keep dragging her deeper into your world, away from me. She kept your company afloat for months while you were deciding if you wanted to keep going, or whatever it was you were deciding. Once she got things turned in a good direction again, you offered her a partnership. And now this. You seem to have some strange hold over her. It goes all the way back to law school. I haven't forgotten."

Billy's blood was flowing again, and he was starting to get agitated himself. He'd never had high personal regard for James Bosken. Outside the courtroom, the guy had all the charm of an accountant at tax time. But Billy had tried to be hospitable because of Claire.

The three of them had drinks a few times, even went out to dinner once after the partnership became official. His opinion hadn't changed. He thought Bosken was in over his head with Claire. She was more woman than he deserved. Billy had told her that once, long ago. Of course, she didn't listen.

"Claire is strong-willed; we both know that," Billy said. "The real problem is that you haven't been paying her much attention. You can't blame me for that. If you ignore your wife, you can't expect her to always be there for you with open arms."

"But she always seems to be there for *you*."

"I pay attention to her."

At that point, Bosken moved closer. His lips were quivering. Billy could sense an escalation coming, maybe even a punch, and he was bracing for it. If he needed to fight before breakfast, right there in his foyer, then so be it.

"I'm going to give you a chance to leave under your own power, James, and I suggest you take it. You go home, cool down, work this out with Claire. You can apologize to me later. Or, if you take a swing at me, I'll leave you laying in my yard and call an ambulance to pick you up. The reporters will love that story."

Bosken took a deep breath and recalculated. He seemed to be having second thoughts.

"If I ever hear that you're messing around with my wife, you'll regret it," he said, stomping to the door. "I mean it, Billy."

"And if you ever come around here again with anything less than an apology, I'll hurt you, James. I promise."

The door slammed shut, and Billy could hear Bosken peel out of the driveway. He walked back into the kitchen, popped a couple of Aleve tablets into his mouth, and stuck his head under the running faucet. What a start to the day.

There was a click as the door to the downstairs opened. Claire peeked timidly around the corner.

"I'm sorry," she said. "I didn't mean for you to get involved in this. I thought he would have cooled down by now."

"I didn't know James had that kind of passion in him. Good thing he didn't see your car in the garage, or things would have gotten messy."

"I'm sorry, again. I really appreciate you letting me use one of your guestrooms. I hated to wake you up like that."

"I'll admit I didn't expect to see you again last night. And I damn sure didn't expect to see your husband this morning. But it'll be okay, as soon as this headache goes away."

"Have any more Aleve?" Claire said with a giggle. He flipped the bottle to her.

"By the way, James said you told him you wanted a separation. You didn't mention that. Is it true?"

"I told him that, but I was pissed off at the time. We just seem to be going in different directions … the chemistry isn't there anymore. I don't know where we're headed."

"He seems to think that you and I have something extracurricular going on, and we both know that's not the case."

"I told him that. He's always been a little jealous of you."

"Then I'm guessing he won't like us running off to Nashville together in a few days."

"He'll have to deal with it," Claire said. "I don't care right now." She walked over to the window and looked out at the water. "I just don't care."

CHAPTER SIXTEEN

The dark-haired beauty settled into her lounge chair and scanned the horizon off Kite Beach.

The thermal winds were picking up, as they tended to do in the heat of the afternoon. Now the kiteboarders were everywhere along the Cabarete coast, knifing through the surf at warp speed, launching themselves acrobatically from the rolling waves as their colorful kites dipped and darted against the backdrop of a cloudless sky.

Wearing a black string bikini, oversize sunglasses, and a Panama hat, the woman turned up her cup and sipped the last of a strawberry mojito. A man was stretched out next to her, face down on a woven straw mat. She tossed a handful of sand on his back and laughed.

"Emmanuel, are you still alive? I have a question."

He rolled over slowly and squinted out at the blue-green waters of the Caribbean. With smooth, bronze skin and black, curly hair, he looked to be in his early twenties. A curious smile appeared on his face.

"How do all those guys keep from getting their lines crossed up, or running into each other?" she said.

"There are dozens of kites out there now. It's amazing. I've never seen anything like it."

"The best kiteboarders in the world come to Cabarete. We have it all here — windsurfing, kayaking, diving, canyoning, horseback riding. Whatever you want. The Dominican Republic is a place for adventure. You like adventure, don't you, Rachel?"

She smiled and jiggled her empty cup. "Another?" he said.

"Best mojitos I've ever had. One for the road."

"Would you like to get in the water first? It is very nice; the surf is no problem. I could see yesterday that you are a powerful swimmer."

"I don't think so. This bikini isn't built for swimming. I'm fine here … just another drink, please. And get whatever you want."

Emmanuel sat up, brushed the sand from his back, and adjusted his red Speedo for the short walk down the beach.

"You never said why you are here," he said. "There are not many American women like you, traveling alone outside the resorts. Where is your man? Are you hiding?"

Rachel gazed out at the kites again. *Good question.* She had been hiding for a while, often in plain sight. Sometimes she just felt invisible.

"Rachel?"

She snapped back to the conversation. "I'm not alone. You're with me."

Emmanuel managed a rueful smile. "So you are hiding with me. I like that. Can you stay longer?"

Her response was subdued. She pursed her lips and shook her head slightly.

"No. It's time to go."

The two had met in the backcountry the previous day. Emmanuel was from Sosua, a resort town up the road a few miles, and worked as a guide for a kayaking company that ran tourists down the Yassica River. He took a special interest in the tall American with the athletic build and distinctive accent. One smile and he was hooked.

He had volunteered to keep her company, show her around on her last day in the bustling beach village. That morning they had joined the swarm of scooters that infested the area, riding up to Sea Horse Ranch before returning to her Beach Palace condo for lunch. She would enjoy his hospitality for just a while longer, and then move on.

"So you are going to Puerto Plata this afternoon?" Emmanuel said. "Would you like me to drive you there?"

"That would be nice. I need to start moving soon, because things can get stacked up at that airport. I've already packed. You can load up my bags at the condo, and maybe I'll give you a little something for being such a good boy." He raised his dark eyebrows. "For now, just another drink. Please."

The Mojito Bar, serving legendary drinks and sandwiches, was about halfway down the row of open-air restaurants that spilled out onto the beach. Rachel handed Emmanuel a hundred-dollar bill and admired his musculature as he shuffled away and disappeared into the crowd.

Rachel leaned over to grab her tote bag from the sand. It took a minute to dig out the Orange cell phone and slip of paper. She removed her sunglasses and squinted as she tried to read the screen in the blazing sun.

The stream of vendors hawking trinkets to tourists along the shoreline was picking up. She waved off another, a weathered woman carrying a case of jewelry, as she tapped out the number on the paper. A man selling cigars was right behind, and Rachel shook her head again.

After several seconds, she heard the voice on the other end.

"Hello, it's me," she said. "I'm going to be heading your way soon and hoped we could get together again. Would you like that?"

CHAPTER SEVENTEEN

B illy had spent the last few days pondering the new direction of his business, talking with trusted advisers, doing the research, trying to calm his nerves.

He had to admit that he liked what he saw and heard. Trepidation had turned to confidence, his natural state of mind. Premier Sports and Entertainment would be a player to be reckoned with sooner rather than later. He was sure now.

By the time he arrived in Nashville with Claire and Jackson Warner, their assistant, Billy was in full-blown public-relations mode — a dashing, charming force of nature straight out of the Great Smoky Mountains. From Dolly Parton's hometown, no less. They'd appreciate that in Music City.

Billy wanted to impress Ty Nelson and any of his musical acquaintances that might be in the market for fresh, new representation. Time to get the word out.

To help the cause, Billy had invited not one but three of his NFL clients to join the party. It was the middle of the offseason and they were glad to get away for a couple of days and help him. They'd make quite a splash at the Bluebird Café.

Billy was especially anxious to see Jarvis Thompson. The wide receiver for the Miami Dolphins had already blossomed into one of the top young stars in football. He had helped to lead his team to the playoffs for the first time in seven years. He was Billy's protégé, a high-profile client in the nation's most high-profile sports league, the one who gave the agent undeniable credibility, and he had come a long way in a short time.

Even the look off the field was different. The player's long braids were gone, and so was the ever-present stubble on his face. He was wearing a tailored sport coat and jeans with Italian loafers, a very Miami vibe. Jarvis was a pro now in every sense of the word.

Also invited were Leroy Mitchell, the mammoth offensive tackle of the Atlanta Falcons, and Jeff Spangler, a backup quarterback for the hometown Tennessee Titans. Spangler was a fairly accomplished guitar player in his own right and could be spotted in several Nashville honkytonks during the season. As it turned out, he had even struck up something of a friendship with Ty Nelson.

All three players would be good pitchmen for what Billy and Claire were selling.

The Premier group had rooms at the Omni Hotel and a limo ride out to the Bluebird. Claire looked radiant as usual, poured into a pair of white jeans and a shimmering sleeveless top, but she paced nervously in high heels as she waited in the lobby.

"Are you okay?" Billy said.

She smiled. "I just want tonight to go well. We're going to get some good publicity. I want everything to be perfect."

"Don't worry, it will be. You look fantastic, by the way."

Billy turned to Jackson, who was quietly playing a supporting role. "Have you talked to the players?"

"They're on their way down, hopefully not all in the same elevator. Leroy needs his own elevator."

Jackson was a whip-smart kid with strawberry blond hair and a quick wit, another graduate of the UT law school who always seemed to be right in sync with Billy. Claire had hired him about a year before to run the office, and he had become a valuable asset as he transitioned into an assistant's role. Billy trusted him implicitly and treated him like a little brother.

Within minutes the group had gathered near the main entrance. Big smiles and hugs all around as they anticipated a fun evening. The camaraderie that Billy worked so hard to build was easy to see.

"Somebody seems out of place here," said Mitchell, always the joker. "The pretty one."

Claire giggled. "You can come along anyway, big man."

The driver walked into the lobby and escorted them out to the black Hummer stretch limo. The drive would take about fifteen minutes, he said, unless traffic backed up, which it often did. The Nashville traffic was getting worse by the week, it seemed.

"So this is your town?" Mitchell said to Spangler, his booming voice filling the cabin as they pulled away from the hotel.

"Backups don't have towns," the quarterback said, and they all laughed. "I'm actually a Wisconsin guy, but Nashville is a nice place to live for several months out of the year. People are friendly here, they love their football, and they really love their music. It's a great mix."

"So you know Ty Nelson?"

"We've talked a little bit. He's a big Titans fan, and I've seen him play at a couple of places downtown. Excellent musician, real nice guy. Just a good ol' Tennessee boy. Hope that translates well out in L.A."

Claire spoke up. "Ty's a perfect example of what's going on here. He can play any style of music and appeal to any audience. If you've seen the early Songmasters segments, you know what I'm talking about. He stands out in a crowd."

"He's right where he needs to be," Spangler said. "There's so much music talent here, songwriting and performing, it's ridiculous. And most of the time, even with all the growth, Nashville still feels like a small town dressed up like a big city. There's an energy that's different than anywhere else I've been. Night after night, any one of these bars could have somebody singing or picking a guitar that will blow you away. Male or female, young or old, doesn't matter. I like to walk down Broadway and just take it all in. It's one big show."

"Well, I'm in awe of real musicians," Billy said. "You know I play the guitar from time to time. Garage-quality stuff."

"You sound pretty good after a couple of beers," Claire said. "Maybe several beers."

"Thanks, partner."

"It's interesting what you and Claire are trying to do with the business," Mitchell said. "I like the idea of mixing the ballers and the pickers."

"Claire gets the credit, or the blame, for that. And it's not just pickers. All sorts of performers. There's room for us in the market, and we're ready to go to work and see what happens. This looks like a good place to start."

The limo pulled up to the Bluebird Café and the group filed out. There wasn't much to see from the outside. The unassuming club, with less than a hundred seats, was located in a strip mall on Hillsboro Pike. No frills. Of course, all sorts of music legends — Garth Brooks, Sheryl Crow, John Prine, even Steven Tyler — had played the Bluebird through the years. Taylor Swift was discovered there as a fifteen-year-old songwriter.

Ty Nelson was hoping to follow their lead.

"This is it?" Mitchell said. "With all due respect, it don't look like a music shrine to me."

"It's what they call an *eclectic* place," Claire said. "Let me go inside and see what's happening." A few minutes later the door opened again and she waved the group over.

"Ty and his sister aren't here yet, but one of the guys who works the sound said some seats have been reserved for us. There aren't a lot to begin with, so let's settle in and get comfortable. This should be a special treat."

CHAPTER EIGHTEEN

The group was still waiting for Ty to arrive when Jarvis sidled up beside Billy. "Let's talk for a minute," he said. They walked toward the back and stopped. The buzz of the crowd was growing.

"What's up?" Billy said.

"I just wanted to mention that I'd spoken to Russell Mann on the phone, like you asked."

"What did you think?"

Jarvis shook his head. "Not the most talkative guy. I thought we'd have something in common right at the start, working with the same agent and playing ball in Florida. I mentioned that I'd like to come up to Orlando and watch him play sometime. He didn't seem too interested. Said the season was almost over and he wasn't sure where he'd be next year."

"I told you he wasn't Mr. Personality. I was just hoping you guys could make some sort of connection for down the road, for what it's worth. I'm trying to help Russell as much as I can, draw him out a little more. I like to think of it as a team effort."

"You know I'm glad to help when I can. By the way, I talked to a couple of other people I know there in the

Orlando area. They're big Magic fans, season-ticket holders who really follow the team close. They said Russell has built kind of a reputation in the community. Some of it has been smoothed over here lately with the team winning and him leading the way."

"Reputation?"

"Just that he's a New Yorker and seems to have a big chip on his shoulder most of the time. He's made the team tougher, for sure, but he ain't changed much off the court. I know a lot of cats that come from the streets, but I've heard them New York streets is different."

"Cats like you?"

"I have to work hard at it every day, putting the past aside. Running the streets is a way of life, and some never get it out of their systems. You need to be careful with Russell. You've got a lot riding on him."

"Careful? In what way?"

"You're a smart guy, Billy. Just watch yourself is all I'm saying." Jarvis chuckled. "Russell is no stranger to trouble, but you aren't either. It has a way of finding you."

That brought a big smile to Billy's face. Jarvis knew what he was talking about, better than anyone, even Claire.

The men had an intimate connection, going back to when Jarvis was still a kid trying to play his way out of the projects in a small town in the Florida panhandle. He ended up at Tennessee to be close to Billy and developed into the most heralded receiver in college football. He was taken second overall in the NFL draft, signed a big contract, and hadn't looked back.

But his rise to stardom in Miami almost didn't happen. Late in his final season at UT, Jarvis went from can't-miss prospect to infamous kidnapping victim, taken from Billy's own dock by mobsters in the middle of the night. They were trying to settle an old score for their boss. It was messy.

The agent led a rescue effort that freed Jarvis weeks later, but the highly publicized drama continued to follow both men. Billy suspected that it always would to some degree.

"Speaking of trouble," Jarvis said, "whatever happened to Rachel?"

Billy shook his head. "Don't ask."

***

The Bluebird was filling up, starting to generate the unique vibe it was known for.

The typical show there would bring together three or four songwriters, often up-and-comers, in the middle of the listening room. They'd sit and take turns playing their songs and accompanying each other with instruments and vocals. It was more like an impromptu jam session than a performance, and the audience was always intimately involved. Tonight would be even more so.

The side door opened and Ty eased into the room with Michelle, his sister. He was beaming like a man who had been away from home too long. There was hearty applause and cheers from all around.

They both stopped for a moment to greet Claire, who quickly introduced Billy and Jackson.

"Thanks for coming," Ty said. "I see you brought some serious muscle with you."

The NFL players leaned in and shook hands with the musician. "Good to see you again, Jeff," Ty said. "I look forward to talking with all of you later. Just sit back and enjoy."

The guest of honor waded through the crowd to the center of the room and took a seat with two other men and a woman. He couldn't stop smiling as he reached back and lifted a Taylor koa guitar from its stand.

The appreciative fans grew quiet and gathered even closer.

"Gotta love Nashville. This is home," Ty said, strumming a chord or two and adjusting the microphone in front of his face. "I really appreciate all the support and just want to thank the people here at the Bluebird. When I was a new songwriter on the scene, they let me come and polish my skills and build some confidence out here with some other great musicians. It was kind of a springboard for my career, and I'm thrilled to be back in this room tonight with good friends. I hope to keep making you proud."

The crowd roared its approval.

"Now," he said, "let's play some music!"

Ty launched into one of his most popular songs, Powerball Blues. It was a pure country tune about a woman who had broken up with her boyfriend, only to find out later that same day that he'd won the lottery.

You used to say I was the one, even called me your hero/But life can be a numbers game, baby, and today you're a zero

And away the evening went.

The songs kept coming for almost forty-five minutes, a remarkable ride through Ty's diverse repertoire, before the musicians stopped to take a break. Ty walked back over to his sister, who was sitting with Claire and her group, and leaned down.

"You really look nice, Claire. I've enjoyed our phone conversations here lately. So good to see you again in person."

"Listen, it's my pleasure. We couldn't wait to come down. I've been telling everybody what an amazing artist you are, and apparently a lot of other people agree. I think Billy here is one of them."

"I'm blown away," Billy gushed, sliding his chair closer to the conversation. "Love what you're doing, man, the whole feel of it. I really look forward to talking some more, getting to know you better. Maybe you could even teach me a few of those guitar licks."

"I'd like that, too," Ty said. "The last agent I had, he put me on the right path. But we just didn't click after a while. I need some fresh air around me, and I've heard good things about you. Of course, I've known Claire for a long time. She's a sharp lady. Always was."

Claire blushed a bit and managed a demure smile.

"That's Claire — a hurricane of fresh air," Billy said. "And she's got big plans for you. We both do."

Ty nodded and smiled. "By the way, I'm happy to have these NFL guys here tonight. I'm a big football fan, and I've gotten to know a bunch of Titans in the last year or so."

Spangler, the quarterback, stepped in and slapped Ty on the back.

"Welcome to the team," he said.

"Well, it's not official yet," Ty said, "but I feel good about it. If you'll give me another hour or so here, we'll all head somewhere quiet. There's a restaurant downtown that's one of my favorites. They're holding a room in the back for us."

"Take your time. We're enjoying the show."

Ty eased back toward his seat in the middle of the room. The beer was flowing and his friends were fully invested in their budding star. Everything felt right.

"Thanks again for coming out … the support really means a lot," Ty said as he picked up yet another instrument, a jet-black Gibson mandolin. "We're going to play a few more tunes and then just party a little bit. I'd like to dedicate this next song to the gorgeous redhead sitting over there. Claire is an old friend. And she's my new agent, it looks like. Not bad, right?"

The two smiled brightly amid a few whistles and hoots, locked in each other's gaze for several seconds. It almost seemed that no one else was in the room.

CHAPTER NINETEEN

The car stopped at the edge of the Amway Center complex, and the men stared in awe. The bold arena, with its glass and curves and angles, was immersed in an LED glow at dusk. IT'S A MAGIC NIGHT, declared the marquee on the side of the building. If there was any doubt, the blue-and-white color scheme on the entrance tower served as a beacon to all passersby that Orlando's team was indeed at home tonight and preparing for battle.

The place would be full, twenty thousand strong, to see if the Magic could lock up a playoff spot with a win over Detroit in the last game of the regular season. It had been five years since their last postseason berth, which seemed like an eternity to the team's frustrated fan base.

The driver rolled down his window and took a deep breath of the moist air.

"Don't feel like the Bronx, does it, D?" he said to his passenger in the dark blue sedan. "Definitely don't smell like it. Another world."

"So this is Russell's house? Nice. Wish we could go in and give him our best, see some ball. No way the Pistons will keep him down."

"Like the big sign says, it's a Magic night. I feel it already."

The men laughed and then sat in silence for a minute to collect their thoughts. It had been a sixteen-hour ride down the East Coast, and they had stopped only three times along the way. Briscoe had been behind the wheel for the last five hours.

"Why would a brother who has all this be bringing trouble around for no reason?" Deion said, shaking his head. "Why kill a little man like Blue?"

"You know Russell. He never could keep control. Like that Hernandez dude from the Patriots. Had it all and ended up just rottin' in prison 'til he slipped that noose around his neck."

"Difference is, Russell may not make it to prison."

The car started again and rumbled back toward the interstate.

***

Inside the arena, Billy was standing in front of his seat and feeling the chills. He'd never heard the place louder, and now everyone in the building rose as one.

Orlando was up by a point with less than a minute to go. The Pistons, mired in another losing season, were not rolling over. If the Magic were to punch their ticket to the playoffs, they would have to earn it. A loss tonight and Indiana would claim the final spot in the Eastern Conference.

Russell Mann had done everything in his power to carry his team to victory. His last free throw gave him thirty-two points, and he stood at the foul line to shoot again. The toss rippled the net, and Orlando's lead was two with forty seconds left.

Isaiah Compton, Detroit's crafty point guard, pushed the ball to the other end and stopped and dribbled as the shot clock wound down. Compton got a high screen that freed him for a long three-pointer. *Swish.* A collective groan rolled through the building as Orlando called timeout.

Twenty-one seconds left, season on the line. Coach Jeff Sanders drew up a play in the huddle for Russell to get the ball at the left elbow and drive hard to the basket. If the shot didn't go down, there was a good chance he'd draw contact and a foul. Two free throws would work just as well.

The Magic inbounded the ball to Kenny Scott, who dribbled the ball beyond the three-point line as the clock approached ten seconds left in the game. The fans stood and held their breath.

Scott finally made his move, but the Pistons had pinched Russell with two defenders. There was no passing lane, so Scott was forced to put up a contested jumper from the wing. The ball caromed high off the back of the rim, up for grabs.

Sensing where the miss was headed, one of his intangible strengths, Russell spun away from his defenders and grabbed the rebound. He went back up in a crowd and laid the ball in as the horn sounded.

The place erupted. Russell was quickly buried in a pile of joyous teammates while the Pistons froze dejectedly. Orlando, 105-104. The Magic's season would continue for at least another two weeks.

Billy fell back in his seat and rubbed his face. God, he loved sports. And to see one of his own clients deliver in a crucial game, a do-or-die game, the feeling was indescribable.

Russell's stock was continuing to trend up.

***

The men were able to duck into a parking spot and take a short nap. Now they waited and watched for the black Mercedes SUV to exit the players' lot.

Finally, Russell was cleared through the security gate and headed toward the expressway. The blue sedan fell in behind him.

"Don't look like our man is going home," Briscoe said. "Probably has a little party planned."

"Is he alone?"

"Couldn't tell."

Briscoe and Deion followed the SUV east toward the Milk District for a couple of miles, until it stopped at the curb outside the Hocus Pocus nightclub. Russell jumped out while his passenger came around to the driver's seat to park the car. Billy was waiting on the sidewalk with another handshake for Orlando's all-star. He had to admit, he'd never felt better about Russell's future than he did at that moment.

They went inside, and the cheers started up immediately. Everyone in town knew Russell now; everyone was on the bandwagon. Billy stepped back to let the player enjoy the limelight by himself.

Russell broke out a huge smile and pumped a fist. "Let's keep it going!" he yelled. "Watch out, Greek Freak!"

That brought a hearty cheer from the patrons who recognized the nickname of the star player the Magic would play in the first round.

A waitress escorted the men to a private booth in the back and took their drink orders. Russell wanted a Boilermaker — a glass of beer with a shot of whiskey. Billy opted for a pint of Ocean Sun lager.

The waitress was quick to return, and Billy raised his glass for a toast. "To the Magic and their star forward," he said. "It's a winning combination."

Russell threw back the shot and chased it with a big swig of beer.

"I hope you're not planning to drink too many of those," Billy said.

"T-Bone is my designated driver tonight. He gets to watch me drink."

"Just go easy. You guys haven't won anything yet; you've just stayed alive. There's some serious basketball yet to be played. Milwaukee is going to be a tough matchup."

For once, Russell couldn't stop smiling. "Stayin' alive," he said. "Story of my life."

"You know you probably made yourself a lot of money with your performance tonight."

"Is that right?"

"I saw Larry West after the game, and he seemed ecstatic. You put up the numbers this season, but your team won. That's what it's all about — being a winner. They're going to want to lock you up for several years, keep building around you."

"So how much we askin' for?"

"I've thought a lot about it since our last discussion, and right this moment I'd say one hundred million for four years sounds about right. That's a little more than we talked about. Based on the talent that will be on the market, and where the cap is headed, it's a good starting point for negotiations. Your best basketball is still ahead of you."

Russell took a deep breath and leaned back in the booth.

"A hundred million? Man, that's a lot of zeroes. Think we'll get it?"

"Maybe. The market dynamics are shifting and you're going to be in high demand. Like most businesses, the NBA is driven by supply and demand. And there aren't many guys like you; that's a fact. So who knows? Could even be more, depending on which teams get involved. Not a bad position for a kid from the Bronx."

Russell smiled dreamily and leaned out to look around the club. Things were just getting cranked up.

"We've already discussed most of the details of the contract," Billy said. "You just need to think about winning games now. The rest will take care of itself. Any more questions?"

"Just one: Where's T-Bone?"

CHAPTER TWENTY

The small man found himself face down in the floorboard, wedged between the seats. The stench of the rotting carpet was making him nauseous, but that was the least of his worries.

He had been snatched off the street, beaten, blindfolded, and gagged. His hands were bound behind his back with duct tape. T-Bone was a prisoner.

Briscoe James didn't know where he was going as he drove away from the club. The important thing was that he and Deion were taking control of the situation, imposing their will, just like they would back home. Grabbing Russell Mann's sidekick was a start.

The brothers had yet to decide how it all would end.

"So what are we going to do with him?" Briscoe said. "Before, or *after,* we kill him?"

There was a groan from the back seat, then another.

"I bet this is how they did Blue. Probably didn't know what was happening. Just taken out and dusted and dumped along the side of the road like trash. Turn him over, Deion, and rip that tape off his mouth. Let's ask him."

Briscoe eased into the parking lot of a large shopping complex, drove around to the back, beyond the loading docks, and stopped the car behind a row of dumpsters. His partner leaned over the seatback and reached down to T-Bone, who was breathing heavily through what was likely a broken nose. Even in the shadows, Deion could tell that blood was everywhere. The smell filled the air.

He pulled the duct tape from T-Bone's mouth and pressed the barrel of a handgun against his face.

"What's your name?" Deion said. No response. "Tariq Vaughn. Russell Mann's bitch. That's who you are. Russell seems to like running around with little guys. Must make him feel like a boss."

"You remember Blue Warren, don't you?" Briscoe said. "He was our brother. Half-brother, actually, but close enough. Russell should have known that we'd come. New York, Florida, it don't matter. When you cross the line, shit follows you."

T-Bone tried to clear his throat and speak. He was no stranger to men with bad intentions, but this time he was the one in a vulnerable position.

"I don't know what you're talking about."

"So you're saying you weren't part of it? We know that you and Russell are tight. *We know.*"

"I didn't kill nobody."

"That still don't answer the question. You and Russell were with Blue earlier that night. And I'm pretty sure you were with him later, too. We don't know what all went down, but let me just tell you that my little brother here is anxious to settle the score. And I'm not sure I could stop him, even if I wanted to."

Deion pulled back the hammer of his silver revolver. "Why don't I just shoot him now, and we'll throw him in that dumpster there? Be done with it."

Feeling the cold steel against his temple, T-Bone began to fully grasp the gravity of the situation. He had to save himself.

"It was Russell," he cried out. "I just drove."

The brothers looked at each other and nodded.

"That's what some of the boys thought all along, and now we know," Briscoe said. "How'd it go down? What happened?"

The prisoner swallowed hard. "We'd been drinking at this club, after Russell went off big time against the Hornets. He was jacked. Blue was there, kept talking to Russell's girl, and she just left." T-Bone paused to catch his breath. "I didn't think nothing about it, but you could see it on Russell's face. He called later and wanted me to come back to his house and get him."

"Why?"

"He wanted to pick up Blue, have another drink. Don't know why … Russell can go off sometimes for no reason, like a crazy man. It was late, probably two o'clock, but I called Blue and told him we were coming by the motel. He was waiting outside when we got there."

"Then what?"

T-Bone was lying on his side, and the pain was taking a toll. His breathing had become more labored, his words more uneven.

Briscoe growled. "Then what?"

"We were riding around drinking a bottle of whiskey I'd brought, and Russell told me to drive out of the city. I just went where he said. We got out away from everything, and he finally told me to pull over."

"What was Blue doing?"

"He didn't know what was going on. I didn't either. They were just talking, and Russell started in about his new girlfriend, how Blue had done him wrong and ruined everything. He was jacked up on something. Next thing I know, he's pulling a piece out of this bag and points it right at Blue. I said to myself, Holy shit, he's gonna shoot him."

"And that's what he did?"

"Made Blue get out and kneel in the ditch. Blue was begging Russell not to do it … he still didn't understand. I just sat there behind the wheel, looking straight ahead the whole time. I heard the gun go off. Russell climbed back in the car, all calm, and we went back to his house."

"So you left my brother laying there, rotting in a ditch, and just went back to Russell's big house? Like nothing happened."

"What was I gonna do? There wasn't nothing I could do to stop him."

The brothers took the news calmly at first. It validated what they suspected all along — that Russell Mann had lost his head again, just like he always used to. Except this time the big man would be held to account. They would make sure of that.

Deion leaned down close to his prisoner. "Where does Russell live?"

"Outside town a ways. Windermere. Fancy place, maybe a half-hour from here."

"The address?"

"I don't know, but Whispering Pines is what the sign says. Big houses. There's a street called Osprey. You take a right after you come through the gates and his house is way down at the end. You can tell it because it has a fountain that's lit up in front."

"Are the gates open?"

"I've never seen them closed."

"You have a key to the place?"

"No, but there's touchpads on the front and back doors. You just punch in 2-5-2-5. Russell's jersey number, twice."

"What about cameras?"

"They're up on the walls and around, but Russell never had them wired up. He always said he was going to. I don't guess he ever saw a reason."

"He shoulda, bro."

Briscoe clenched his jaw and nodded at his brother. They both jumped out and opened the back passenger door, dragging T-Bone from the floorboard onto the pavement. Briscoe rolled him over and propped him against the dumpster.

"I didn't know what Russell was gonna do. I swear," T-Bone said, his voice cracking. "He's whacked. You're from the hood … you know he is. He's always been this way."

Briscoe erupted, kicking T-Bone in the head repeatedly until he slumped over.

"That's enough," Deion said. He slapped a fresh strip of duct tape over the man's mouth and pulled him to his feet. "Stand there and look at me, bitch."

Tariq rocked back and forth, wheezing, trying to steady himself like a punch-drunk fighter. As he turned to face Deion, there was a powerful, muffled gasp and the small man dropped to the ground with a thud.

Briscoe had plunged a metal shank into his back, just below the rib cage. He stood over the body, smiling.

The brothers waited in the shadows for the groans to fade away. There was no sense of panic or alarm. This wasn't the first time they had to kill a man to send a message. And it wouldn't be the last.

Deion leaned on a dumpster and lit a cigarette. After a few moments, the only sound in the spring air was the distant traffic. Briscoe knelt down and wiped the long blade on Tariq's jeans. "Get the tarp," he said. "Let's take him for a little ride."

Quickly, they spread the plastic, lifted the body onto it, and rolled it up. The men tossed the bloody cocoon in the trunk and slammed the lid shut.

CHAPTER TWENTY-ONE

More than an hour and a couple more drinks had passed since Russell first wondered why his designated driver never showed up.

The parade of fans stopping by his table to talk, offer congratulations, or snap a quick selfie, had finally let up. A Magic night indeed. But now it was time to move on, refocus. There were more games to play, more thrills to come.

T-Bone hadn't tried to call, and he wasn't answering his phone. Another attempt to reach him kicked to voicemail as Russell walked outside Hocus Pocus to look around. Billy followed him onto the sidewalk.

"Where is he?" Russell said, sounding more annoyed than worried. "He's not at the bar, not in the bathroom. He's not out here smoothing the ladies. He was supposed to park and come right in. I'm gonna stick my size twenty sneaker up his ass when he shows."

"Maybe he was tired and decided to wait in your car. If he couldn't drink …"

"He loves being in the bars, just standing around on booty call. He must have hooked up with somebody. Maybe he's in the *back* of my car."

"Let's see if we can find it sitting around here somewhere."

The lot was overflowing with vehicles, so they started looking. After five minutes, Russell located the Mercedes-Benz AMG GLE63 a block over, locked up tight on a side street that fed out to the highway. T-Bone wasn't in it.

"I don't guess you have another key with you?" Billy said.

"No." The first sign of distress appeared on Russell's face. "What the hell happened to him?"

"I don't know, but it's getting late. I can give you a lift back to your house and you can get your spare. You don't want to leave a car like this sitting here all night. It'll get towed, more than likely."

"I'll just call a limo." Russell said. "There's a guy I use all the time. You can just go on back to your hotel."

"It's no big deal; I'm not drunk. It'll give us more time to talk."

The agent plugged Russell's address into the Google Maps app on his phone, and they began to snake their way out of the downtown in a charcoal gray Kia Cadenza. Russell was spent from the celebration. He reclined the passenger seat all the way back and closed his eyes as Billy searched for a sports talk station on the radio. There would be no more conversation.

Before long, the car came to a halt and Billy tapped Russell on the leg. "We're here, big man."

Russell jerked, like he'd been awakened in the middle of an intense dream. He suddenly sat up and squinted toward his house.

"You know where you are, don't you?" Billy said with a laugh. "I'll just wait while you run in and get the key."

Russell yawned and rubbed his face. "I'm too tired, man. I'm just going to stay here and crash. T-Bone can bring me the car in the morning. You want to stay?"

"I've got an early flight. I need to go back to the hotel and get everything together. I'll be in touch. Got some important things to take care of in Knoxville, but hopefully I'll make it back down here for at least one of the playoff games. It's high times for Magic fans."

"And high times for Russell Mann. *Suuuper Mann!* What was that number you said? *Hundred million?* So many stacks I won't be able to count 'em."

"Let's get this season over with first. Take care of yourself and the rest will take care of itself. Just be smart."

***

Russell slapped his agent on the shoulder and got out of the car without another word. Billy watched the tall figure lope up the sidewalk, past the fountain, to the front door. Russell punched in his passcode and entered.

A text message dinged on his phone just as he shut the door behind him. It was from T-Bone.

In your bedroom.

Russell frowned and glanced outside as Billy was pulling away from the house. He tossed his phone on the bar and hustled down the long hallway.

"What the hell?" he said, leaning into the dark bedroom to flip on the lights. The horror took his breath away. A body, grotesquely swollen and covered in blood from head to toe, was lying there on his white bedspread, hands folded across the chest.

Russell moved closer and then froze. His mind flashed back to another time and place. The first victim.

Russell's father had been carved up in his bed by a battered wife who couldn't take any more. She had waited for him to pass out then took a butcher knife to her tormenter. Ruby was sitting there next to the body, shaking and staring blankly, when their eight-year-old son walked into the room.

Russell lost both parents that night — and whatever shred of compassion was still left in him. His life took a hellish turn. For years the anger and bitterness continued to build, and all the success on the basketball court couldn't ease his pain. He had lost control.

Now it was all coming round again.

Russell yanked open the closet door and grabbed the gun off the shelf. The MAC-10 machine pistol was one of the oldest weapons in his collection, described as "fit only for combat in a phone booth." Russell knew his life might one day come to that. He kept the gun close, ready to unleash its fury at a moment's notice.

Breathing heavily, he began to search the house with the weapon drawn. A trail of blood led toward the back door.

As he followed it, another text pinged in. Russell walked to the bar and glanced at the lit screen.

You next.

The adrenaline rush hit again. He tried to swallow but his mouth was bone dry. He spun around. Nothing.

All the doors were locked. He was alone.

CHAPTER TWENTY-TWO

Russell stood staring through the front windows, his eyes darting back and forth, looking for any movement. The gun felt sweaty in the palm of his right hand.

He was ready for anything, but the night was still, eerily quiet. The storm had passed. Time to assess the situation, make a plan.

Russell didn't rattle easily, even in the face of stunning violence.

The kid from the New York projects had always felt disconnected in the rich enclave, an outsider in class and color. Never more so than now. Mayhem had no place in Whispering Pines, but it had always followed him.

Russell stepped to the bar and nervously tapped out a phone number.

"Something's come up," he said. "I need your help, and I need it now. Get over here and bring a couple of boys with you. Park around back. I'll be waiting."

He made one more pass around the property. Finally, Russell felt secure enough to lay the black gun beside him. He grabbed the bottle of Hennessy off the shelf and took a big drink. Then another.

What to do with the body?

Russell was still pacing in the house when the headlights swept across the front windows. The car pulled to the garage and three men got out. One was approaching when the glass door slid open.

Geno was a giant of a man, perhaps six-foot-six and three hundred fifty pounds. His unpredictable nature made him even more menacing. T-Bone had been one of his best friends.

"What's wrong, Russell?" Geno said. "Didn't sound good."

The player stood silently in the doorway and waved them into the house. They trailed him down the hall and into the master suite. Geno had barely gotten a foot into the room when he stopped cold in his tracks.

"Holy hell. Is that … *Tariq*?"

"Somebody killed him and left him here. Don't know if he was shot or stabbed or just beat to death, but it's a mess. Was laying there just like that when I got home."

"Who? Who did this?"

"I got a feeling. I think it was some homeboys."

Geno edged closer and exhaled a huge breath. He looked back at the men behind him, who were shaking their heads. The smell of death was unmistakable.

"So this didn't happen here?"

"No, he was with me downtown after the game," Russell said. "He was parking my car and never came into the bar. My agent ended up bringing me home."

"Your agent? I hope he didn't see this."

Russell shook his head.

"You got some bad mothers in your neighborhood," Geno said. "They a long way from the Bronx. What brought 'em all the way down here?"

Russell didn't answer. He was starting to put the pieces together in his mind but couldn't make out the puzzle just yet.

"Whatcha want us to do?" Geno said.

"I want you to get T-Bone out of here. Wrap him up in the bedding and put him in your trunk. Burn the body or bury it somewhere he can't be found. Ever."

The men glanced back and forth, their grim expressions showing the doubt in their minds. One of them spoke up.

"I don't know, Russell," he said. "Whatever's going on here, we don't want no part of it. This is serious, man. New York gang shit. No sense getting on somebody's hit list if you don't have to."

"You on that list, bro?" Geno said. "Sure looks that way. Somebody gunnin' for you."

"You don't worry about that," Russell said. "I just need your help right now. I'll make it worth your time."

He walked down the hall and into a back room. When he returned, he had a stack of bills in his hand.

"Five Gs right now to clean up this mess. All of it," he said.

Geno stared at the cash and smiled. "C'mon, Russell. Let's make it ten. And we probably be fools at that."

"Okay, ten. I'll get the rest to you tomorrow, before the team leaves for Milwaukee."

"That's right, you got the playoffs coming. Big man with a big new contract in the works. And here you got a dead man in your bed. This could blow up your world."

"That's why I'm counting on you, Geno. Get this place cleaned up, and then never another word. We good?"

Geno turned to his cohorts and nodded. He glanced back down at the bed. His friend was hardly recognizable now.

He took the corner of the comforter and flipped it over T-Bone's face.

"Little bastard was always headed for trouble. Let's wrap him up. Least he'll be easy to carry."

"Let me know when you're done; I'll be out front. Make it quick."

Russell handed over the cash and hurried out the door as the men went to work. He pulled the phone from his jeans pocket and stopped in the yard, next to the fountain. It was usually a peaceful patch of green space where he could feed the koi, or just stand and take his mind off things. Not tonight.

Russell pressed the phone to his face, scanning his property from one side to the other, looking for any movement. All quiet.

"I got a problem here, and I need to know something," he said. "When's the last time you saw the James brothers?"

PART TWO

CHAPTER TWENTY-THREE

There wasn't much doubt in Claire's mind that it would be a good weekend in Los Angeles. Maybe a great one.

The Songmasters competition was ready to resume at the Patrick Center, and Ty Nelson was going to be one of the four finalists standing at the end of the week. Claire could feel it.

She was checking messages and getting ready to make the drive to Nashville when Jackson leaned into her office.

"You and Ty flying out together?" he said.

"And Michelle, too. Feels kind of strange."

"How so?"

"I don't know … it just seems like a new chapter in the making. Exciting, I guess. This could be an important week for the business. I'm already fielding all kinds of requests for Ty, and if he makes it to the last week it's going to get wild."

"I hope you're good luck," Jackson said. "That's a seriously talented bunch he's up against."

"You've been keeping up with the show. What do you think of his chances?"

"Well, there are three country types, and you have to think at least one of them will make the finals. The chick is gorgeous, but I think Ty is the most talented. He has some great covers and is a hell of a guitar player. He can elevate his game."

"Let's hope so. I'll keep you guys posted on how things are going."

Jackson went back out to his desk to answer a call. The front door swung open and Billy waltzed in with a pleasant smile on his face.

"You ready to go, girl?" he yelled back.

"Leaving right now."

"So you and Ty are traveling together? Does James know?"

Claire waved Billy into her office and shut the door. He could tell he'd struck a nerve. "I was just kidding," he said. "How is James anyway?"

"I don't know … we're officially separated. He's renting a place at Crystal Falls."

"Wow, I'm sorry to hear that. Maybe some time away will do you both good. You know what they say about absence."

"Right. Makes the heart grow fonder. I'm not feeling it right now."

"Tell me if there's anything I can do. Seriously. You know I just want you to be happy."

A rueful smile came across her face. "I should have listened to you years ago. Anyway, I need to get going. I'm meeting Ty and Michelle at the Nashville airport."

"Safe travels. And stay in touch. We'll be watching."

Claire slid her tablet and phone into her shoulder bag and headed toward the door. With the red hair, pearls and sleeveless blue business dress that showed off a figure hard-earned in the gym, she was a force to be reckoned with.

Billy was caught looking as she stopped abruptly and turned back around. "Do I look all right?"

"You look fine. Doesn't she look fine, Jackson?"

"Yes, indeed. Finer than fine."

"By the way, I've already been contacted by a couple of other acts in Nashville that have some major potential," Claire said. "One of them is a spinoff group that used to tour with Alison Krauss. Endless Journey. They're good friends with Ty, and I think they might like to be friends with us. How does that sound, Mr. Beckett?"

"Like I said, bringing musicians into the fold was a great idea."

Claire shook her head and waved as she went out the door. Billy and Jackson waved back and smiled at each other.

"She's a badass," Jackson said.

"Yes, she is. And I know she thinks highly of you as well. You two have gotten tight."

"Yeah … I appreciate her giving me a chance here when she did."

"I don't know if I've told you lately, but you're doing a great job. There's a lot more going on right now, and I want to get things restructured for the long haul. That certainly involves you."

Jackson had hoped to follow in Billy's footsteps since back when he was just starting law school. He used to spend his free time hanging around the office, learning the art of representing elite athletes from the agent's perspective. Now he was firmly entrenched in the business.

Billy appreciated the youngster's drive and enthusiasm for any task that presented itself. This morning, however, Jackson seemed a bit off his game.

"The three of us will sit down soon and talk at length," Billy said. "I just want you to know that Claire and I appreciate what you're doing, and that we're thinking about things. PSE is a work in progress, but I like the direction things are taking."

"Sure. Thanks."

Billy patted him on the shoulder and headed back to his office. His cell phone rang, and he plopped down behind his desk.

"Hey, Dad, what's up?"

Franklin Beckett sounded flustered. "I hate to bother you, son, but that damn dog has run off. I've been looking everywhere for her."

"Lucy?"

"Yeah, she saw a squirrel or something and bolted out the side door. I've been walking around the neighborhood for a while, yelling for her with a piece of turkey in my hand."

Billy chuckled. "Have you tried steak?"

"No, and I'm running out of time. I just got back to the house and she's not here. I really need to get on to work; I've got meetings this afternoon. I don't know what you can do about it. Guess I just wanted to vent, since this is really *your* dog."

"Tell you what, I've got a little time to spare. Why don't I come out to Sevierville and see if I can help. I'd like to see you anyway. I'll be there in half an hour or so. Keep looking in the meantime."

Billy jumped up and headed toward the door.

"Crisis?" Jackson said.

"Just the next one in line. My father has lost track of his dog. I remember when I was the one who couldn't keep up with his pets. We'll talk again soon, I promise."

Jackson nodded and watched the boss hurry off.

CHAPTER TWENTY-FOUR

Billy drove slowly along the tranquil streets of his youth, circling one block and then another, scanning the yards of old friends. The memories streamed through his mind.

The Becketts used to rule the neighborhood back then. Franklin was a police officer working his way up the ranks, and his wife Anna, the tireless community servant, was always at the forefront of a new fundraising drive or civic project. Their boys were star athletes, seemingly destined to do wondrous things in the sports world. Those were the days.

Billy made one last loop in his Escalade toward the back of Oak Park. No sign of Lucy. He finally pulled into the driveway of the modest brick ranch, beside his father's red pickup truck.

He walked through the carport and into the house.

"Any luck?" Billy called out.

Franklin was sitting on the couch in the den. His head was resting in his hands, and he seemed winded from his latest search.

"Nope, but maybe it's just as well. That dog has been testing me lately, and I've had about enough. Good riddance."

Billy placed a hand on Franklin's shoulder and smiled. "You love her and you know it."

"Seriously, it's a hard dog to love. She's either scratching up the doors or shredding paper all over the floor. Hell, anything that comes out of the printer, she grabs it and runs. She doesn't listen to anything you say, won't even look at you most of the time. And if you give her half a chance, she's out the door. As far as I'm concerned, she can just stay out there with all the other wild animals."

The miniature goldendoodle definitely had more poodle arrogance running through that twenty-five-pound body than golden retriever sweetness. She was Billy's dog to begin with, a gift from Rachel King when the two were still living together in Knoxville. Both relationships had gone astray.

Lucy needed more companionship, more time and attention, than Billy had been able to give so Franklin took her in.

"I'm guessing she'll turn up," Billy said. "We'll surely see her before we see Rachel again."

"What's the latest on that search?"

"Still no word. Her parents will keep looking for her, regardless. It's sad."

"That's a real shame. I liked Rachel. I wish things had turned out different for everybody."

"So do I, Dad. And we still don't really know what the story is. It probably won't have a happy ending."

Billy glanced out at the street. "At least she left us a deranged dog to remember her by. Seems appropriate. There's not much else to speak of."

"Except that black leather outfit with the whip that's hanging in your closet." Billy blushed. "But that's another story, right?"

"And not one I'm going to tell."

Franklin let out a big laugh and a slight grimace crossed his face.

"Something wrong?" Billy said.

"Nothing really. I've just been feeling a little pain here and there lately."

"What kind of pain?"

"Something in my chest. I usually feel it when I cough. Or laugh."

"So you have a cough, too?"

"No big deal."

Franklin was a burly man with a crew cut and bushy mustache that was becoming grayer by the day. He was old-school cool. Billy had never known anyone cooler under pressure.

"Anything else?"

"Just a little tired right now. Chasing after that dog didn't help."

Billy's brow furrowed. He had become increasingly protective of his father, even though the ex-Marine never needed much protection.

It had been just the two of them since John committed suicide almost two years ago. He shot himself on the pitching mound where he had been a high school All-American, distraught over the fallout from his involvement in the Jarvis Thompson kidnapping. John was on the phone with his older brother that morning when he pulled the trigger.

I love you, Billy. Tell Dad I love him, too. Please forgive me.

The call would haunt Billy forever, and so would the look on their father's face when Billy had to deliver the devastating news. Franklin had never gotten over the death of Anna. And suddenly he had to bury their youngest son.

"How long have you been feeling like this?" Billy said.

"A few weeks, maybe a month."

"Don't you think you should go have it checked out?"

"Already did, yesterday. I was in for my annual physical and mentioned it. Dr. Kilday sent me for some tests."

"And?"

"Haven't heard any more about it. I guess everything checked out, or else they don't know yet. No big deal."

The doorbell rang and Billy got up to answer. He flashed a broad smile as soon as he opened the door. Jeff Mullins, a friend from the down the street, was holding Lucy in his arms. It looked like she was smiling, too.

"Come in, Jeff," Billy said.

"Thought you might want this one back. I knew Franklin was looking for her, and I saw her run past my back windows. I grabbed some meat, like he said, and started calling her."

Lucy still had dirt on her nose, and her curly, cream-colored coat was littered with debris.

Franklin snickered. "Couldn't you have at least brushed her before you brought her back? I wish you could experience that. Brushing that dog is like brushing a badger."

"Sorry, but you're on your own now," the neighbor said, setting Lucy free on the floor. "Good luck."

"Thanks, Jeff. I really appreciate it."

"Well, another problem solved," Billy said as he shut the door. "Now, about those test results. You're tougher than an old piece of leather, but I still want you to call me as soon as you hear something."

"No need to worry. Are you heading out of town?"

"I'm going to be at home tonight, working on some business stuff with Jackson and watching the NBA play-offs. The Magic are playing at Milwaukee."

"That's a tough draw. Getting the top seed in the first round usually means a quick exit. It's almost automatic in the NBA. Your man will have to play out of his mind to keep Orlando in the series."

"And that probably won't be nearly enough. But it's been a great year for Russell, regardless of how it ends."

"Sounds like he's gonna cash in."

"Soon."

"Good for you. Thanks for coming out, son. Sorry it was a waste of your time."

"Coming home is never a waste of time. Wish I could do it more often."

Billy glanced down at Lucy, who looked like a little angel curled up in Franklin's favorite chair.

"Sure you don't want her back?" Franklin said. "I'll pay you to take her."

"Tempting offer, but no thanks. I have to run. Let me know."

CHAPTER TWENTY-FIVE

A bad day was getting worse for the Orlando Magic and their star forward. The team was playing catch-up in its series opener in Milwaukee. The Bucks had bolted out to a big lead early behind their MVP, the six-foot-eleven phenom Giannis Antetokounmpo, and showed no signs of being reeled in. They had hounded Russell Mann into a poor shooting performance and led by fifteen to start the fourth quarter.

Earlier in the day, rumors surfaced on social media about another unsolved murder case — a drive-by shooting that left two men dead in a seedy area of Orlando. *Could Russell have been involved with this one, too?* That's what someone acquainted with the men had anonymously thrown out there. The rumors were gaining traction on Twitter and the Magic message boards. So far, there had been nothing from police.

"Here's a new tweet," Jackson said as he reclined on Billy's couch, scrolling down the screen of his smartphone. "It says Russell looks pretty dead himself tonight."

Billy downed the last of his Heineken and popped out of his chair.

"Idiots," he said. "They're everywhere now. I think we've seen how helpful tweets are, from the president on down. Did we really need to create a new way for people to spout off? It's embarrassing."

"No doubt that we've become a culture of drama queens. As you know, some of the Twitter things tend to build momentum for a few days at least, whether they're true or not. We may be hearing trash talk about Russell for the rest of the playoffs. After that, who knows? It could be more than just embarrassing."

"There's never a good time for scandal, but this is the worst. We're so close."

On the television screen, nothing good was happening. Russell turned the ball over for an easy Milwaukee score. Bucks by twenty. Timeout, Magic.

Billy shook his head disgustedly and grabbed the remote control, muting the sound.

"Damn, he *does* look dead. Welcome to the playoffs, Russell." Billy turned to Jackson and tried to offer perspective. "The spotlight is a lot more intense, and every possession counts. A player has to be there and feel it to understand it. But Russell has always played better when he's backed into a corner. He'll come out fighting next game — figuratively, of course."

There was a long silence before Jackson said, "You don't think there's something to these rumors, do you?"

"You're asking me if I think Russell, our most important client in the NBA, is capable of murder? Or at least being involved?" Billy paused again, like he was trying to convince himself. "No, I don't. He's not *that* stupid."

"It would be a hell of a scandal, maybe bigger than the thing with Jarvis."

"Thanks for putting that into perspective for me, Jackson. I don't know if the business could take another hit like that. My sanity damn sure couldn't."

Billy walked toward the kitchen. "Want another beer?"

"No, thanks. I probably need to get on home. There are a couple of things at the office that need my attention early in the morning."

"Have you thought any more about what we discussed? I want to funnel some of those accounts your way, let you take the lead. Things are moving fast and we need to stay up to speed."

Jackson nodded. "I know. I'm just weighing some things right now."

"What kind of things?"

There was an uneasy expression on Jackson's face. "To be honest, I'm looking into a job offer out on the West Coast. I've been waiting to tell you. I have a good friend from school, really smart guy that started up a new business near Seattle, and it's doing very well. He keeps calling me, trying to get me interested."

"What kind of business?"

"It's called InnerSpace. They buy up entire floors in old office buildings, wholesale, cut them into smaller spaces and do these really cool build-outs to lease. It's creating little communities of young entrepreneurs all around Seattle. Sounds simple, but they've built a great business model and need some more legal minds as they expand down the West Coast. Everything I've read about the company says it's one of the hottest start-ups out there right now. It's getting a lot of buzz."

"Leasing office space? Really? That doesn't sound like you, Jackson. I thought you wanted to be an agent to the stars. Dealing with the sports gods. Walking around in the best arenas and stadiums and ballparks in the world. A new adventure every day. You're on a good track here."

"No shortage of adventure, for sure. This offer is just something I need to think about. I have the inside connection, and my friend told me yesterday that it was my last chance to get in, kind of take it or leave it. It'd be a fresh start, something new. I've lived in Knoxville my whole life, so a change of scenery might be good."

Billy was taken aback. He'd never envisioned Jackson just packing up and moving. That would be a significant blow to their operation at a time when everything was ramping up.

"Again, I want you to know that Claire and I are expecting big things out of you. We like having you around. You've gotten to be like family, a little brother or something. You can't just bail on us."

Jackson stood, almost choked up, and smiled sheepishly. He patted Billy on the shoulder and headed to the door.

"I'll let you know," he said. "See you in the morning."

CHAPTER TWENTY-SIX

The phone call came in early. Jackson was already sitting at his desk as Billy walked into the office. He held up a finger and parked the call.

"It's a woman," Jackson said. "She wouldn't say who she is, but she has an accent."

"What does she want?"

"She just asked for you. Want me to take a message?"

"I'll take it. Leave her on hold for a minute."

Billy stopped at the coffee pot and filled a mug.

"I think I had a nightmare last night," he said. "Russell played like a dog and his team got its doors blown off. The fans were laughing at him, taunting him at the end of the game, and he ran up in the stands and just started punching people like a wild man. It was total chaos, like that Malice at the Palace thing in Detroit several years ago. I woke up in a cold sweat. That didn't really happen, did it?"

"I'm afraid the first part did. Game one was an official beatdown — Bucks by twenty-three, if I recall. The Greek Freak was amazing. The good news is that Russell didn't punch anybody, didn't incite a riot, and there's still more basketball to be played."

"Any more brilliant tweets this morning?"

"Of course. The Twitter universe never rests, and the way Russell played didn't help the situation. The haters are always ready to rise up. He has to know what's being said out there."

"He does, but there's an oblivious quality about him. I woke him up on my way in this morning. He says he wasn't involved in any murder, doesn't care about tweets, and isn't worried about anything other than winning the next game. Typical Russell. He leaves the worrying to me."

Billy shook his head as he stirred some cream and sugar into his coffee. "There's plenty to worry about." He eased into his office and stared at the phone on the desk for a couple of seconds before picking up.

"This is Billy Beckett."

"I saw something, Mr. Beckett." The voice had a nervous pitch; it was definitely a Hispanic woman.

"Excuse me. Who is this?"

"I saw what your client did."

"What are you talking about, miss?"

"Russell Mann. The basketball player."

"I really don't have time for games this morning."

"No games. I saw Russell in the car with his friends that night. I was there."

Billy's mind turned immediately to all the rumors. *The double murder in Orlando.* Could she be the source, how it all began? Or just someone looking to capitalize?

"Tell me who you are and we'll talk," he said.

"I'll talk and you listen. I want you to understand what I'm saying. I'm serious here."

He took a deep breath. "Okay. Let's hear it."

"Me and my friends were sitting in a car down in Parramore that night. It was late. We knew Russell was coming. He wanted to spend some time with me, and my boys were looking out for me. I'm not a cheap date, you know? A black car pulled up alongside. There were two men in front, and I could see Russell in the back. He had a big smile on his face."

"You saw a big smile in the middle of the night?"

"I did."

Billy remembered reading the newspaper accounts. There *was* a woman in the car. She had told police that she was asleep in the backseat when gunfire erupted, shattering the windows. She reportedly rolled over into the floorboard and held her breath until the shooters sped away in a dark sedan.

When she finally sat up, the story went, her friends were slumped over in the front seats. Police speculated that they were the latest casualties in an ongoing turf war between rival gangs. Such shootings were becoming common in that area.

"So these men wanted me to get in their car," the woman said. "They didn't want to pay the premium rate. My boys didn't like that — there ain't no discounts that time of night — and they started yelling back and forth. Next thing I know, the guy who's driving pulls out a gun and starts shooting. I still have glass in my hair."

Billy wanted to hang up but couldn't.

"This isn't the story you told police," he said.

"I could always change my story. I'm scared for my life, you know. The cops will understand. If I tell the truth, your boy will be going to prison instead of signing a new deal. He won't be trolling down here in the middle of the night anymore. That's for damn sure."

"Are you trying to blackmail me?"

"All I know, Mr. Beckett, is that you're his agent, the man who looks after his money. You got a lot to gain if Russell Mann signs that contract. If he goes to jail for murder, you're both losers. Follow me?"

Billy was almost speechless. "I'm not sure. What do you want?"

"I just want you to understand about Russell. He's a dangerous man, and he's playing a dangerous game. And I don't mean basketball. I'll let you know what it's going to take to keep me quiet. It won't be long."

With that, she was gone.

CHAPTER TWENTY-SEVEN

B illy sat back and tried to digest the information. *Was he being conned?* It didn't sound that way. *Should he report the call to police?* That could only add fuel to a fire that might otherwise burn itself out quickly.

He didn't see much purpose in furthering the investigation of his client, who was already being tried by some in the court of public opinion.

The ring of his cellphone broke Billy's train of thought. His father was calling.

"Good morning, Dad. How are you feeling?"

The reply was not reassuring. "I don't know, son. Kind of strange."

"What do you mean? Have you heard back from the doctors?"

"I just spoke with Dr. Kilday again. I'm still trying to process it. He says the X-rays show something in my lungs. He's giving me antibiotics and wants me to see a specialist."

"Something like *what*?"

"Maybe pneumonia. Could be something worse, even mesothelioma. Big word, right? We just don't know."

"Isn't that *cancer*?"

There was hesitation. He could hear his father breathing heavily on the other end, and his own breath quickened as he tried to understand.

"It's, uh, something that gets into the lining of the chest," Franklin said. "They say it could have been caused by exposure to asbestos fibers, maybe decades ago. It's rare, but firefighters are more susceptible. In fact, they're twice as likely as normal people to get the disease. I've been on a few fire scenes with those guys myself."

"I can't believe this. If it's mesothelioma — and surely to God it isn't — what's the prognosis? How do they deal with it? *How can I help*?"

"Slow down, son. I just know if you've got to get cancer, this probably isn't the one you'd pick. I've known a few men who battled it through the years. But let's not jump to any conclusions just yet."

Tears began to well up in Billy's eyes. "I'm coming out there right now," he said.

"There's no need, Billy. Really. I'm getting ready to go to the office and take care of some things. I'll be coming to Knoxville anyway to see a specialist that my doctor recommended, maybe as early as tomorrow, and we'll talk then. It may take a little while to know exactly what's going on."

"And I'm going to be right there with you every step of the way. I want to know every detail."

"You will, I promise. Let me get on with my day here, and I'll see you soon."

Billy tried to collect himself and be strong. "I love you, Dad." The words never had more meaning.

"I love you, too, son."

Billy dropped his phone on the desk and stared blankly at the floor. Another blindside hit.

Franklin had always been a pillar of strength, in good times and bad. He was a big man with a big heart. Invincible, it seemed.

He and Billy had carried each other emotionally through the devastating losses, first with Anna and then John. Billy had been so distraught during one stretch that he was ready to give it all up — his business, his close friendships. Franklin helped him pick up the pieces and keep moving forward.

But how would they get through *this*?

Billy looked up to discover Jackson standing in the doorway with a look of concern on his face. He always seemed to be tuned in to his boss. This time the distress was obvious.

"It's Dad," Billy said quietly. "He may have cancer. They don't know yet."

"*Cancer?* God, that's terrible. What kind of cancer is it?"

"Maybe mesothelioma. It has to do with the lungs, and it's really bad news."

"I'm so sorry. What can I do to help? Anything."

Billy grew dark. "That's the question, isn't it? What can anybody really do to help anybody else? We're all on a ticking clock, waiting for our time to come up. If it's not one thing, it's another."

Jackson didn't know what to say. He stood silently as Billy took a deep breath and tried to compose himself.

"The woman who was just on the phone," Billy said. "I want to know who she is. Call up the story on that

Orlando shooting and see if the reporter identified the woman in the backseat of the car the two men were killed in. I need a name."

"I'm on it. Shouldn't take but a couple of minutes."

Billy leaned back in his chair and rubbed his face. He suddenly felt numb.

Russell Mann's brewing troubles suddenly didn't seem so urgent.

CHAPTER TWENTY-EIGHT

The specialist in Knoxville was out of town and couldn't see Franklin for a few more days. He wanted more tests done.

In the meantime, the stoic police chief had gone back to work, carrying on like nothing was wrong.

Billy had spent the last couple of nights in Sevierville, making sure his father had everything he could possibly need after work. He really just wanted to be close. By the third day, there wasn't much he could say or do.

Nothing new had arisen about Russell Mann. The Orlando police were quiet; they were still investigating the shooting. The social media chatter had died down, for whatever reason. Billy was thankful for that.

On the basketball front, the Magic now trailed the Bucks, two games to none in the best-of-seven series. Russell had yet to play up to his regular-season standards, and time was quickly running out.

Billy planned to be in Florida for game four — perhaps the Magic's last gasp — but his father's situation had put the trip on hold.

He walked out the back door and sat down in the white porch swing that his father had bought for Anna years ago. The paint was cracking and the supporting chains had begun to rust, sure signs that Franklin never came out here anymore. The house was like that in a lot of respects; painful memories were everywhere.

A warm breeze whistled through the row of tall white pines along the back of the property. Billy could remember when they were just eye level and still in play in the makeshift baseball outfield.

He turned his phone over and over in his palm. He had been fielding business calls all morning, which helped take his mind off of his father's illness. Now everything was quiet.

For the last hour, he found himself wanting to talk to Derek Woodson, Russell's old AAU coach in the Bronx. They hadn't spoken in a while, and Billy could use some reassurance. Woodson was perhaps the only man who could give him that.

Finally, he scrolled down his contacts and tapped the screen.

"Hello, Derek," he said. "This is Billy Beckett."

"Well, my favorite agent," came the reply. "Long time no hear, man. How you doing?"

"Things could be better. But they could always be worse, right?"

"I hear that. Looks like our man Russell's season is about over, but he's had a hell of a run."

"I don't think either one of us predicted he'd be in this position just a few short years ago. Rags to riches. It's quite a story."

"I always knew he had the talent and the guts to make it in the NBA. There was no doubt about that. It was just the other things."

"That's why I'm calling, Derek."

"Something wrong?"

"I don't know. We're just getting close to free agency with him, maybe the most important stretch of his whole career, and sometimes I think I'm losing touch. He can zone out in a hurry."

"I know what you mean," Woodson said. "Russell's a hard kid to figure at times. He's got his own way of doing things, and it don't always make sense. I'm sure he's full of himself right now, too, which only makes things worse."

Billy began rocking back and forth in the swing.

"That's putting it mildly. You're the one guy who seems to be able to get through to him, and I just wanted to hear your take on things. Have you talked to him lately?"

"He used to call me fairly regular, but it's been a while. I usually just get his voicemail when I call him, so I don't try much anymore. Is there a problem?"

"Again, I don't know. I'm just trying to understand where his head is. It's always been a struggle."

"I've said it before, Billy, but you deserve a lot of credit. No one else wanted to help Russell at a time when he needed help. You got him in the league and stayed behind him. I know he wouldn't be where he is now without you."

"I appreciate the opportunity this job gives me to kind of steer guys like him," Billy said. "The money is ridiculous, of course, and it's easy to lose one's way. I guess what I'm wondering is whether Russell would be foolish enough to throw all that away. I keep hearing things."

"What kind of things?"

"I don't want to get into the details, but I'm concerned. He's got a bodyguard, some guy with a gun, around him all the time now. He keeps telling me not to worry."

"You know his background, how everything kind of went to hell when he was young. He was there the night his mother stabbed his father to death. She went off to jail and Russell went to live with his grandmother, poor woman. He just ran loose after that. It's been a long, hard road."

"What do you think he's capable of, Derek?"

The bluntness of the question startled Woodson. *"Capable of?"*

"Do you think he could turn violent, get angry enough to really hurt somebody?"

"Are you asking me if he could *kill* somebody?"

There was a pause. "I guess that's what I'm asking," Billy said. "How *dangerous* is Russell Mann, in your opinion?"

"I'm not real comfortable going there with you, Billy, but I will say this: he's a kid with a lot of anger penned up inside. I don't know if that ever goes away. I understand that you're in a tough position as his agent, and I wish I could make you feel better about things."

"But you can't?"

"No. I'll just leave it at that. I'm always glad to talk to you, but I'm afraid Russell is past the point of listening to me. You're the man with a direct hand on his life, and a lot of what happens with him — good or bad — will be up to you. I hope in a few years we can all look back and be satisfied with the results."

Billy thanked Woodson and stuck the phone in his pocket. The old swing moved back and forth gently, the rubbing of the chains sounding like a slow metronome. He could almost feel his mother's presence as he rocked.

CHAPTER TWENTY-NINE

The seven musicians stood nervously on the stage. Four men and three women, arm in arm under the bright lights. The audience held its collective breath.

The announcement of the last finalist for The Songmasters was at hand.

Ty Nelson's supporters looked on nervously. They had been remarkably calm the last couple of days, through the rehearsals and preliminaries in Los Angeles, and it seemed to rub off on their man. Ty was captivating with his performances — pitch-perfect vocals, seamless guitar licks, commanding stage presence. He was a star among stars, and the judges had treated him like one up to now.

But there was no room left for error.

Three of the finalists had already been named, including Lori Green, an eye-catching brunette who used to back up Kenny Chesney. She was a shoo-in from the start. Would another singer with country roots make the cut?

Everyone in the theater waited breathlessly with the national television audience.

"And our fourth and final contestant to move on to The Songmasters grand finale next week is …" The emcee drew out the suspense with a long pause. "Ty Nelson!"

There were hugs all around on stage, and the man from Nashville stepped forward and let out a big sigh of relief. The other finalists joined him as the house band played, spotlights rolled, and the audience cheered. Classic show business.

Claire embraced Michelle and Ty's parents, and then fell back in her seat, emotionally drained.

"Amazing," Michelle yelled. "Can we take another week of this?"

"I don't know, but we're going to see."

Within minutes, Claire's phone was vibrating. It was Billy, who had been watching at home in Knoxville.

"I think you've got a winner there," he said.

"*We've* got a winner. I told you he was a big-time talent."

"Good call. He's definitely shining tonight … pretty heady stuff for his agent. I saw a shot of you sitting there with his folks; you looked excited."

"Couldn't have a better end to the week."

"When are you coming back?"

"I'm going to stay an extra day here with Ty, just to help him get things in order for next week. He's going to be busy. His family is taking an early flight out in the morning. How about our man in Orlando?"

"Looks like Ty's going to outlast Russell. This series has sweep written all over it. We can start worrying about what's next for him."

"Yeah, I've been keeping track." Claire got up and walked into the concourse. "He doesn't seem to have his A-game. Anything going on in Knoxville?"

"Jackson has been holding down the fort — we need to talk about *him* soon — because I've been spending some time in Sevierville. Dad isn't doing too well."

"What do you mean?"

"I'll tell you about it when you get back," Billy said. "Just tell Ty that we're all proud and looking forward to the finals. I like his chances. That boy has a great career ahead of him."

"We just need to get him through this next week and see where things lead. I'll be in touch soon."

Claire put away her phone and noticed that Ty was in a group hug with his family on stage. They were all beaming as photographers snapped pictures. He waved Claire up and was waiting with open arms.

"I'm really glad you're here," he said with a big smile.

"So am I. Billy's jacked, too; I was just talking to him. He wishes he were here but said to tell you he's with you in spirit. All the Tennessee people are."

"I guess we're a real team then. And we're in the finals. That calls for a little celebration."

***

The group floated through the hotel lobby and stopped at the elevators to catch its collective breath. Midnight was approaching.

"That was a great evening," Michelle said, leaning on her brother. "You were amazing, Tyler. I always said you were the most talented one in the family. But I'm still the smartest."

"I'll give you that," Ty said. "I wouldn't be standing here without you — all of you. It means a lot that you were able to share this ride with me. And it's not over yet."

Blaine Nelson, Ty's father, glanced at his watch. The banker wasn't used to being out late, and the euphoria of the occasion was wearing off. He was already looking ahead to the workweek back in Tennessee.

"Son, I wish we could just hang out in Los Angeles for another week," he said, "but I've got all kinds of things piling up at home. If everything goes well, we'll try to make it back for the last show."

"Of course we'll be back," his wife, Joyce, said pointedly. "You know we wouldn't miss it for anything."

Ty laughed and hugged his family a final time. "Have a good flight and I'll check on you late tomorrow. Love you. Tell everybody back home hello for me."

The elevator opened and the Nelsons filed in. Claire was about to follow but stopped when Ty gently reached out and touched her elbow.

"Hang on just a minute," he said, waving to the others as the door closed again. "Want to have a nightcap? We can talk some more."

Claire seemed a bit startled but was feeling no pain, no inhibitions. She was still caught up in the moment.

"Sure. Why not?"

They walked down the corridor to the hotel bar and settled at a table in the back. There were just a few customers scattered about, and it took a minute for the cocktail waitress to notice them.

"Bring us two glasses of your best champagne," Ty said.

"Sorry, sir," the waitress said, "but we don't sell champagne by the glass."

"Okay, a bottle then. Best you've got. And please open it for us."

"Really, Ty?" Claire giggled. "That should sit well with Jack Daniel's."

"Doesn't everything? I just wanted to tell you again how much I enjoy having you with me. It's an old fantasy, I guess."

"Fantasy? How so?"

Ty cocked his head with a devilish grin and tried to imagine the scene. He could already feel the heat radiating between them.

"You know you're gorgeous," he said. "I've always wondered what it would be like …" He was almost afraid to continue. "I'd love to have you come up to the room, but I don't want to cause trouble. I know you and your husband are separated."

She took a deep breath and exhaled nervously. "That's only part of the problem. It's a bad idea to get intimately involved with clients. That's what all the agent manuals say."

"So I'm just a client? That hurts. I thought we were old friends."

"You know what I mean. I really like you … it's just that judgment can get clouded in a hurry. You want me clear-headed and at my best when we're making decisions about your career, don't you?"

Ty smiled seductively as the waitress stopped with the open bottle, a napkin tied around its neck, and two crystal flutes. "Best we've got tonight," she said. "Veuve Clicquot Yellow Label."

"Good enough." Ty filled the flutes and handed Claire one.

"Let's don't worry about my career," he said, raising his glass to toast. "I just want you at your best right now. Here's to a very enjoyable collaboration. I can't wait to see how it turns out."

They each took a sip and Ty signed for the room charge. He stood and extended his hand. He was becoming more irresistible by the minute.

"You're an incredibly beautiful woman," he said.

"I think you already said that."

"I hope you don't mind. Why don't we take the bubbly upstairs? Forget the manuals, just kind of go with the flow."

Claire looked at him carefully before taking his hand and rising from her chair with a dreamy smile. Her natural defenses were gone.

"Maybe this once," she said. "For old times' sake."

CHAPTER THIRTY

ew serious NBA observers had expected Orlando to put up much of a fight against the powerful Bucks, and it now looked like the sweep was inevitable.

The surprise to many, however, was Russell Mann's performance. Even if his youthful team wasn't yet up to the challenge, the star forward figured to be a singular force, maybe carry the Magic to one win along the way. And then he'd head into the offseason as one of the most coveted free agents in the league. That was Billy's hope.

Russell hadn't followed the script; he had been erratic in three lopsided losses. Analysts blamed inexperience, not used to being in the thick of playoff pressure — him or his team. They simply weren't ready for prime time. It was part of the maturing process.

Whatever the case, Russell had struggled mightily to recapture the magic of the regular season. Not only were his scoring and rebounding averages down, but his intensity had also dropped off. He almost seemed distracted, and he had quit talking to reporters. That only made matters worse.

Billy couldn't help but wonder about any number of things himself as he leaned forward in his seat at the

Amway Center. The agent was feeling pressure from all sides.

NFL camps weren't far off, and that's where the majority of his business was done. His clients got antsier, needed more attention, as each day passed and another grueling season drew closer. Good thing he had Jackson to help ease their minds. But for how long?

Billy had managed to push his concerns about Holly Grace to the back burner. She was in the middle of the busiest stretch of her season and had been calling less, which was probably a good thing. He still harbored a certain amount of guilt in getting so emotionally involved with her to begin with, and it was compounded by Rachel's possible interest in the golfer.

The woman most on Billy's mind at the moment: Angel Rivera.

She was the one who was in the backseat of the car in the Orlando shooting, the one who allegedly had seen Russell that night, just a few feet away. Jackson had dug around and managed to come up with her name. For all Billy knew, she could be in the building now, watching them both.

Was she telling the truth?

The Magic were down by twelve at halftime and, unless something changed dramatically, looking at their last half of basketball in a long season. For Billy, the end had a bright side. Absent any more surprises, the focus on Russell would shift to where the forward would be playing next season.

The sooner that deal was done, the better.

New contracts couldn't officially be extended until early July, so there were still several weeks of waiting ahead. But for unrestricted free agents in Russell's situation, it often was a mere formality by the time the signing period began. The courtship was over, the numbers had been crunched, and it was just a matter of putting pen to paper.

Then the hard part — living up to expectations on a grand scale. Russell would be part of an elite club of NBA players who were paid to carry the load night in and night out. The national attention those guys received was relentless. How would he handle it?

Out on the arena floor, the season was rapidly getting away from the Magic now. The Bucks had upped their advantage to nineteen points after three quarters. The building was mostly quiet; some of the more casual fans were already filing toward the exits.

Billy had also seen about enough. He got up and walked into the concourse to make a call. As always, Jackson was quick to answer in Knoxville.

"Looking like the end there," he said.

"Yep. Not the finish we were hoping for, but not a big shock either. I just wondered if you'd heard anything from Claire."

"No, but she should be back in town by now. I think her flight was supposed to land a couple of hours ago."

"I'm still getting her voicemail," Billy said. "Maybe she hasn't thought to switch off airplane mode. She seemed kind of ditzy when I spoke with her this morning."

"Guess the whole thing with Ty is turning out to be a big deal. It's a lot to think about. He's going to be a difference maker as a client, even more so if he wins this thing.

There will be a recording contract, appearances, maybe a national tour. It's the start of something exciting."

"I know you've been fine-tuning things for some of our people. Anything unusual pop up that I need to know about?"

"There is one thing, but not with a client. I'm reluctant to mention it now."

"What is it?"

"It's about that job in Seattle." There was a long pause. "I've decided to go for it."

The news caught Billy completely off guard. He struggled to respond.

"Jackson, we really haven't had a chance for the three of us to sit down and talk about your situation. I wish you'd wait until then before you make up your mind. You want to make the best decision for your career."

"I've been thinking a lot about it and just decided it's time to make a move. It's like I said before; I need to get out and see the world a little more. I really appreciate all you and Claire have done for me."

"So you're packing up and leaving? Just like that?" There was no response.

"I really think we should discuss this when I get back," Billy said. "I'll be in Knoxville by noon tomorrow; we'll have lunch. Keep an open mind."

"It's all I've been thinking about. I just need a change. I'm trying to be up front with you."

"So there's no talking you out of this?"

"I don't think so, Billy. I'm sorry."

"Well, I'm not willing to take no for an answer, especially on the phone from hundreds of miles away.

You know me. And I don't think Claire is going to let you get away that easy either. Don't rush into making a decision you could regret. I'll call you when I get home and we'll go from there."

Billy didn't give Jackson a chance to decline. He slipped his phone into the lapel pocket of his sportcoat and turned back toward the arena. The crowd was flowing heavily against him in a dejected march to the exits. The Magic's season was almost over.

CHAPTER THIRTY-ONE

Almost an hour had passed by the time Russell finally emerged from the Orlando locker room and began to lope down the long corridor.

He wore a pair of baggy jeans and a plain white t-shirt, with Skullcandy headphones pulled down around his neck. His face was blank. No sign of disappointment. No sign of anger. Nothing.

For the last week, the big man's trademark scowl had been missing in action, and so was his competitive edge. It was obvious.

Billy approached Russell from behind and patted him on the shoulder. "Tough finish to a great season. Forget this series … you and your team should be proud. It was a big step up, for both of you."

Russell shook his head and growled something unintelligible in his agent's direction. He kept walking through the bowels of the building toward the players' parking area. Most of his teammates were long gone by now, probably already home thinking about summer vacations. All that remained were security officials and workers who were busy transforming the building into a concert venue. Ed Sheeran would bring his chart-topping act to town in a couple of days.

Billy was anxious to talk, but he knew from experience that it was best to stand back and let professional athletes simmer after losses, get it out of their system. They needed time to clear their minds. Especially at the end of a long, grueling season.

The NBA had been cranking for more than six months now, and it was still weeks away from a conclusion. By then, the Magic's surprising run to the playoffs would be long forgotten by most of the country. But their star forward's exploits would not get lost in the shuffle. Russell had made his mark.

"Let's chill somewhere," Billy said. "We can get a beer if you want. Somewhere quiet."

Russell never broke stride. "I don't know, man. I may just head on home. I'm tired."

"No need to rush things, but we've got a lot to think about. The offseason is here, and it needs to be a great one. It *will* be a great one."

"I just ain't feeling it right now. Let's talk tomorrow. You can come out."

"I have to fly home in the morning; I've got some business to take care of that can't wait. But we'll stay in close touch while you unwind. I'll be back down here soon. You have any big summer plans?"

"Not yet. Once we get this deal worked out, I may go somewhere it's not so damn hot."

"New York?"

"No. Somewhere I can relax. The big city ain't it."

The men walked past the guard station at the exit and stepped out into the night air. It was unusually warm.

They got to Russell's SUV and stopped again.

"Can you drop me at my rental?" Billy said.

"Sure."

Russell eased around to the front of the building and parked next to the white Infiniti. Billy started to open the passenger door but then hesitated.

"One thing before I go; I can' t get it out of my mind. Do you know a woman named Angel Rivera? She lives down here."

Russell didn't flinch. "I don't think so. Why?"

"I'm not exactly sure. She called me at my office a few days ago and told me an amazing story. Claimed she was in the backseat of a car somewhere near downtown late one night when shooting broke out. The two men who were in the front were killed."

"Why tell *you?*"

"Let me finish. She said four men had pulled alongside their car. There was some conversation about her … *services*. And then the gun came out and all hell broke loose. She ended up sprawled out in the back floorboard. Said she still had glass shards in her hair from the ordeal."

Billy spoke slowly and tried to gauge Russell's reaction. There was no giveaway.

"Why you telling me this, Billy?"

"She said she saw someone familiar in the back of that other car, clear as day." Still nothing. "It was *you* — apparently come to hook up with Angel. She knew you were coming."

"That's bullshit. She's lying. I was at home, asleep. I got witnesses."

Billy stared at his client in amazement, unsure how to proceed. He was quiet for several seconds.

"Did I say what night it was?"

"Doesn't matter."

"It was actually the night Holly Grace drove up from Fort Lauderdale and we all went out after the game. As I recall, you left the club with your friends and said you were going home. There were four of you. Black car. Remember?"

"And that's what I did. She's lying, I told you. Maybe the other guys went down there, but not me. How do you know her name anyway? Did she tell you that?"

"No, I just went to the Orlando newspaper website. The story identified her from the police report. Angel Rivera. She had told the cops that she didn't see anybody in the other car, that it was dark and she hit the floor when the glass shattered. Apparently, there's been a lot of gang violence in that area. This just sounded like more of it to the cops."

"What did she want?"

"She said she'd get back to me. I'm surprised I haven't already heard from her again. I can tell you right now, Russell, she's going to want some money to stay quiet. A lot of money."

"I told you I wasn't there."

"You sure?"

"No way."

Billy took a deep breath. "All I know is if she changes her story with the police, we have a huge problem. You're either involved in a shooting, a double murder, and your career is over if you're tried and convicted. Or, if you're innocent, your name gets dragged through deep shit. And that's no good either. I don't have to tell you how that would affect your market value. Why would this woman want to do that?"

"It's a shakedown, plain and simple. She's a hooker and we had some fun together one night. Just once."

"So you *do* know her. And she knows you."

"I'm an easy target. You have to believe me, man."

"Why, Russell?"

"Because you're my agent and you got a lot riding on me. Millions. You're *tied* to me. Tight."

Billy swallowed hard and looked across at his client. Again, he wasn't sure just what to make of the big man. The conversation with Derek Woodson, Russell's old coach, entered his mind.

He's a kid with a lot of anger penned up inside. I don't know if that ever goes away.

Finally, Billy reached over and opened the passenger door.

"I'll let you know when I hear something," he said, sliding out of the SUV. "I'm sure it'll happen soon. It's better for Angel to call *me* than the police to call *you*. In fact, they'll just come out to your big house and pick you up. Probably invite all the media. It'll be a hell of a show."

"You can't let that happen."

Billy shook his head disgustedly. "I need time to think about all this. In the meantime, you need a vacation. Go get on a plane, fly somewhere for a few days. Anywhere."

CHAPTER THIRTY-TWO

Russell was barely a mile down the road when his phone rang. He plucked it from his console and glanced at the caller ID.

"Talk to me."

"Something's going down," came the response. "There's a dark-colored car behind you. He jumped on your ass soon as you pulled away from the arena. It's who we been looking for."

"You sure?"

"New York plate."

Russell locked on to his rearview mirror. There were a lot of headlights shining in his eyes. *Which ones were following him?* The adrenaline began to flow.

"Brothers?"

"Looks like it. Be cool. We're not far behind."

"You know what to do. I'm gonna head toward home and then turn off the main road before Windermere. There's a park near one of those lakes a few miles up. I used to run my dog there. Should be dark and quiet this time of night."

He grinned at the thought. "Let's see if they go along."

Russell exited off I-4 onto Conroy Road, and several cars followed. A few miles later there were only three, spaced out but still within eyesight of each other. He turned to the northwest and slowed as he approached the generous slice of wooded green space that cozied up to Turkey Lake.

The brothers also slowed and kept watch. When Russell went into the park, they followed.

"I'm going to go down to the end and stop," Russell told his cohorts, who had edged onto the shoulder before the entrance. "Doesn't look like anybody's around. You still with me?"

"We're here."

Russell pulled into a parking spot, casually rolled down the windows and turned off the engine, waiting. As expected, the lot was empty and dimly lit. He wasn't sure why, but a smile started to creep across his face. Maybe the rush reminded him of his youth, though he was far removed from the hardscrabble streets of the Bronx. This was an old game in new territory.

Within a minute, the blue sedan had pulled up beside the SUV. Deion James leaned his head out the window.

"Need some help?" he said.

"Thanks, I'm good."

Deion raised his weapon and leveled it at the NBA star, who didn't seem terribly surprised or rattled. "No, you're not."

The door opened and the younger brother sprung out. Briscoe threw his car in park and ran around to the passenger side of the Mercedes.

They looked for potential trouble — police, joggers, someone walking their dog. There was none. The woods served as a buffer between them and the street.

"Russell Mann, for real. You remember us, don't you?" Briscoe said. "I know you remember our brother. He always thought you were one of the best players to ever come out of Hunts Point. Talked about you all the time, especially after you said you'd get him a ticket. And what did you do? Shot the man in the back of the head and left him lying in a ditch."

Russell had no response.

"You knew we'd come, big man," Deion said. "We been watching you."

"So the famous James brothers — fresh out of prison, I hear — drove all the way down to Florida just to watch me? And you didn't even call for tickets. I thought you came to kill T-Bone. That *was* you, wasn't it?"

Deion was starting to get agitated. "He deserved what he got. How did he look, lying there on your white bed? Funny, we didn't hear anything about that on the news."

"I didn't notice."

"Don't be throwing shit around. We can all be honest with each other at a time like this. You're a big man, but it ain't gonna matter. Not here. Not now."

"I'd say it's a bad night for the Magic, wouldn't you?" Briscoe said. "Got knocked out of the playoffs, and now they gonna lose their best player."

Russell suddenly let out a laugh. "You boys never were the smartest. Didn't you wonder why I'd drive up here into this dark park instead of going home? And you just followed right along, made it easy. Should know better, coming from Hunts Point. Always watch your back."

The brothers straightened up and looked at each other curiously. Before they could move again, there were two muffled pops. They fell to the pavement and the night was still again.

Out of the shadows came one figure, crouched and moving slowly toward Russell. Then another, moving in from the other side of the car. A third approached from the back.

Russell stepped out and looked down at the dead men. He nodded approvingly.

"That's twenty grand — ten for each, just like we said," he said. "Ain't no more of 'em, are there?"

"That's it," said the man nearest Russell. "We'll collect tomorrow. Let's get the hell out of here."

"First, there's one more job that needs to be done. I want to tell you now. You interested?"

"You got the cash, I'm interested. Tell me."

"There's another person trying to put the squeeze on me. I can't let her do it. She needs to follow these boys to hell."

"*She?*"

"That's right. Name is Angel Rivera. She's a hooker who lives down in Parramore. It's rough like home, but the Puerto Rican women are different there. Florida Puerto Ricans."

"And you want Angel gone?"

"All the way. And I know how you can draw her out into the open. She can't resist a big payday. Should be easy. We need to go; we can talk tomorrow."

"Be sure to go by the bank, big man. And you might want to run that car through the wash. Before the blood dries."

Russell turned and got back in his Mercedes. By the time he cranked the ignition, the men were nowhere to be seen.

He backed out and hesitated for a moment to survey the scene. Just another peaceful night in the Orlando suburbs, it seemed. His headlight beams swept over the bodies as he sped away.

CHAPTER THIRTY-THREE

Jackson was leaning on the railing of the veranda and staring out at the water when Billy wheeled into the driveway.

As he approached the garage, the agent knew something wasn't right. It was the body language. Even from a distance, he could tell his protégé was anxious.

Billy grabbed his laptop and travel bag from the back of his Escalade and closed the garage door. He quickly turned the corner of the house.

"What are you doing here, Jackson?" he said. "I thought we were going to meet for lunch in town. I know Claire would like to join us. She's not going to let you just walk away without weighing in."

"I talked to her this morning."

"And?"

"She definitely weighed in. She wasn't happy. It made me realize that I need to put everything out there, make a clean break, the sooner the better. I needed to come and meet with you face to face, get this over with."

Billy stopped in his tracks, his bag at his side. "Get *what* over with?"

163

Jackson was becoming emotional. Misty-eyed, he began wringing his hands. Billy had never seen him that way.

"What's wrong, Jackson?"

"I need to tell you something, and you're not going to like it. In fact, you're going to hate me."

"*Hate you? Why?* Is it something more about this other job? I told you to wait until we had a chance to talk."

"That's not it." Jackson took a deep breath and turned to look Billy in the eye. "It's about Rachel."

Billy's bag hit the ground with a thud. "*Rachel?* What about her? Have they found her?"

Jackson walked to the end of the veranda. His eyes darted nervously as he turned toward the lazy Tennessee River. There was a lump in his throat, and he looked like he wanted to run down to the dock and jump in, just disappear under the water's surface.

Billy was close behind now. "Jackson!"

"I've seen her. A couple of times."

"What do you mean? *You've seen her?* Where?"

"She stopped by my condo, out of the blue. There was a knock and I opened the door and there she was. I really didn't know her, but she said she just wanted to talk. I was shocked, but I let her in. I shouldn't have."

Billy couldn't believe what he was hearing. "And you didn't say anything to me? *Why?* You know we've all been looking for her. What reason could you possibly have?"

Jackson slumped into a chair and began rubbing his face with both hands. His breathing was becoming raspy.

"She wanted to know about *you*, where you were and what you were doing. I didn't want to tell her. And then …"

There was a pause. "And then *what?*" Jackson felt the heat of Billy's glare.

"She wanted me to help her, give her information. I've heard how Rachel can be when she wants something. Before I knew it, she had me. I can't believe I let it happen … I'm so sorry, Billy."

"What did she do, Jackson? Tell me now!"

"She seduced me, right there in my own place, and then threatened to use it against me. I'm still not sure how it happened. But I couldn't bear the thought of deceiving you any longer. It's been eating at me since the first day. That's why I'm here now."

"And that's why this job in Seattle has suddenly come up?"

Jackson nodded sheepishly. He choked on his words.

"I can't live with myself over this … I have to get away. I don't deserve the opportunity you and Claire have given me. It's all I ever wanted, and I just threw it away. For nothing."

"I can't believe what you're saying. What else did you tell her?"

"She wanted to know about Claire, your relationship. And Holly, when the two of you were together. That's what really seemed to interest her. It was more that than anything else."

"Why did she want to know?"

Jackson shrugged and continued to look away. Tears welled in his eyes.

"I don't know."

"Where is she now?" Billy said.

"The last time I saw her was a couple of weeks ago. She had called from somewhere in the Caribbean and said she wanted to see me. A couple days later she was here, at my place again."

"And?"

"It was almost like she was toying with me. She was nice until I told her I couldn't help her anymore. She threatened me, and then she went down the other road, reminding me why she was so hard to resist. Like some sort of living, breathing drug. And I'm a fool."

Billy turned away and tried to stay composed. It wasn't easy. This revelation ripped at his heart.

"Of all the people I know, Jackson, you would have been the last I'd expect to stab me in the back. The *very* last. Was it worth it? Was she *that* good?"

There was no answer.

"It's hard to know the damage you've done. And it's not just me and our business, which has already gone through so much just to survive. What about Rachel's parents? They've been agonizing over her disappearance for more than a year."

Billy clenched his jaw and grabbed Jackson by the collar. "I should beat the hell out of you right here and now."

"I don't expect any mercy," Jackson said, bowing his head. "Go ahead, punch me out, throw me in the river. I won't resist. I deserve it."

Instead, Billy let go and began to pace on the veranda, unsure of what to do. His hands were trembling in anger. Finally, a deep sigh.

"It's time for you to leave," he said, "while you still can. If I ever see you again, I don't know what I'll do."

Jackson got up and walked slowly toward his car. Before he got far, Billy called out. "Why is she doing this, Jackson? Tell me that."

The young man stopped and wheeled around.

"I don't know," he said. "I really don't. But you might want to talk to her father again. I got the impression he had something to do with Rachel leaving Charleston in the first place. It's just a feeling."

For a moment, Billy seemed more disillusioned than furious. "You should have told me. We could have put this to rest a long time ago."

CHAPTER THIRTY-FOUR

gent Orange rounded the bend in the Tennessee River and rumbled down the stretch. The stadium loomed large in the distance.

Billy throttled back his boat as they approached and stared in reverence at the iconic home of the Vols. As a boy and later as a UT student, he had spent many a fall Saturday in Neyland Stadium, supporting his team. He couldn't help but think of his late brother and their father. So many memories.

For the last few years, up until last season, he was making the trip regularly down the river as part of the Vol Navy. Cruising on the houseboat that Bradley King had once owned was one of Rachel's favorite things to do.

There was some rich irony in that now.

Billy put *Agent Orange* in neutral and looked over at his partner as she popped the tops on two Heinekens in the cabin.

"I remember sitting up there a couple of years ago watching the Georgia game with Jackson," he said quietly. "We won on a Hail Mary touchdown in the last minute. You remember? Great game in another not-so-great season."

Claire smiled wistfully. She had been at home preparing to return to Los Angeles when Billy called and wanted her to come by his place. There wasn't much conversation on the ride down the river, after he delivered the stunning news. Neither of them could find the words.

"I really don't know where to even start with Jackson," Claire said, finally. "There are so many questions, so many layers to the story. I'm mad and sad at the same time."

"It starts with our business, that's where. We need to reassess."

"How so?"

"We've been giving Jackson more work, more responsibility, and that's obviously out the window now. It's hard to trust anything he was involved with, so I'm going to have to back up and look at all those accounts."

"I don't think there's anything wrong with Jackson's work. He just got caught up in something else."

Billy's eyes widened. "Something else? Is that what you call backstabbing the people who have looked out for you? This is *something else*, all right. It's hard to take."

"We just have to deal with it and move on," Claire said. "What else can we do?"

"We can't afford to take a step back. Going forward, we may need to find another partner. That's something I wasn't planning for."

"We've talked about David Noel down in Nashville. He's good, but I don't know if he's ready to commit to what we're doing full time."

"There are chemistry issues, too," Billy said. "Everybody has to be on the same page, fit together. It's a team effort. That's what I always liked about Jackson. For a young guy, he was really dialed into what we were trying to accomplish. He fit in. Guess I didn't know him that well after all."

"He did good work. Really smart, conscientious, enthusiastic. I enjoyed working with him, and I always thought he felt the same about us. How he could get drawn into this bizarre tryst with Rachel ... it's unbelievable."

"I think it's safe to say he was in way over his head. He's young and naive. Shows the power of beautiful women, right? We never learn."

Claire couldn't suppress a soft laugh. "You're being charitable. To be honest, I'm surprised you were able to let Jackson just walk away unscathed."

"So am I, now that I think about it. Guess I was in shock." Billy eased the boat into gear and took a long last look at the stadium before turning back toward home. "I trusted him completely."

"So what about her father?" Claire said. "You think there's anything to it?"

"I don't know, but nothing should come as a complete surprise at this point. Bradley may have somehow put this whole odyssey with Rachel in motion without even knowing it. Or maybe he does know. I'll find out soon enough."

The boat began to pick up speed again. The sun was getting lower in a cloudless sky, and it reflected in Claire's dark shades. Her silky red hair whipped about that exquisite face.

There was always something comforting to Billy about having her beside him. She had been there so many times.

"So back to L.A. in the morning?" he said. "Think Ty's going to win?"

"He seems pretty pumped. He actually told me yesterday that I was his lucky charm. We'll see."

"You *like* him, don't you?"

"Sure. He's a good guy. And he's going to be a great client for us. People just enjoy being around him. He has that *it* quality. Very marketable."

"I know he's a good guy. That's not what I meant."

She turned away.

"I just hope you're getting some leads from all this," he said. "We're late to the game and having to play catch-up."

"I'm making lots of calls, and you'll be amazed. Believe me, we're going to be moving fast once we get past this with Jackson."

Billy crossed the wake of a passing cruiser and opened up the throttle.

"Men just have so many problems," Claire said. She took a big swallow of her beer. "I used to think it was ego, but now I think it's a lot of innate things. Insecurities with women, for sure."

"That's pretty random, wouldn't you say? By the way, anything new with James? I don't suppose he's back in the house."

"No, that's probably not going to happen. Or else he's going to be in the house and I'm going to move. We just don't connect anymore. I hate to say it, but looks like the end."

"I'm sorry."

"Don't be. It's all right."

"I never did see how James filled the bill there to begin with, but it's none of my business. You never listened anyway." He winked.

She reached out and patted his shoulder. "I should have."

"I just hope I don't see him again in the morning, like last time. I hate fighting before breakfast."

"I'm with you, captain."

Claire lit up the cabin with that beautiful smile and walked out onto the bow of the boat, creating a striking silhouette against the setting sun. For a brief moment, everything was good again.

CHAPTER THIRTY-FIVE

B illy was up early the next morning. He had tossed and turned all night and was still mulling the fallout when he walked into the office to begin damage assessment.

In some ways he regretted not punching Jackson, or at least throwing him in the river, just for the satisfaction of inflicting some real humiliation. There was a time when he probably wouldn't have felt that way, but it had long since passed. Betrayal had taken a heavy toll in his life over the last few years. It couldn't be tolerated.

On the other hand, he knew well what Rachel was capable of. Jackson was just another hapless victim, another mark in her wake.

On the desk, piled high, was a stack of folders — clients whose accounts had been handled by the young attorney. Billy was committed to sifting through them all, one by one, just to put his mind at ease. As if that were possible.

He couldn't help but think about Jackson's last words. *What about Rachel's father? What more did Bradley King know about his daughter's disappearance?* Perhaps more than he was aware of.

"You okay?"

Billy looked up to find Candace, his secretary, standing in the doorway. Her glasses were perched on the end of her nose and there was the usual air of impatience. She kept the office running, kept everybody moving in the right direction. She didn't know about Jackson yet.

"There's a woman on the line that wants to talk to you," she said. "Wouldn't give me her name."

"I'll take it," he said, and quickly picked up the phone. "Billy Beckett."

"Hello again, Mr. Beckett. It's been a few days. Did you think I wasn't going to call back?"

"Oh, I figured you would. Angel, isn't it? Kind of a misnomer."

"I'm not sure what that means, but it's not important. I just wanted to let you know that I've decided what it'll take for me to keep my mouth shut and leave my story the way it is. No cops, and you and your basketball player sign a new contract and go on with your rich lives. Simple."

"Tell me. How much?"

"One million, Mr. Beckett. One million dollars and you'll never hear from me again."

Billy got up and closed the door.

"So you're blackmailing Russell for a million dollars?" he said. "I thought you said it was simple. You know that would not sit well with the police."

"Who's going to tell them? Not you."

"You can't be sure."

"I have the truth on my side; I know what happened. Your player was involved in a shooting. My friends were killed. There has to be a settlement for the victims, and I'm the only one left. I'm collecting for everybody, but I won't say a word. It's really a bargain for Russell."

"My client says he had nothing to do with the murders. He was at home asleep when that happened. He has witnesses."

"He's lying, and I'm sure it's not the first time. I told you that I was waiting for him that night. He wanted to see me. And I did see him, just not the way we planned. I can prove it."

Billy took a deep breath and rubbed the stubble on his chin. He had given this a great deal of thought, at least until other looming debacles began to command his attention.

What to do now?

"I'm going to have to think about this, Angel. A million dollars is a lot of money. You understand that?"

"Here's what you need to understand," she said, growing annoyed. "I'm not a patient woman. I like to do things quickly, get them out of the way and move on. It's my nature. I know Russell has plenty of money. And he's about to get a lot more. He can afford to buy a little insurance."

"For the sake of this conversation, let's say I accept your hypothetical, that my client was present when this incident occurred. And you have acknowledged that Russell wasn't holding a gun when you saw him in that car, so he likely wasn't the shooter. How do I know that you won't be back asking for more money down the road? There's no guarantee this will go away if he pays you off. How can I trust you?"

She laughed. "You can't, Mr. Beckett. I'm a hooker — a damn good one, but not someone men can trust. I'll admit it. Unfortunately for you, your client has put you in this position. I don't know you personally, but I imagine it would be hard for you to sleep, whether Russell pays or not. You need to make it easier on yourself. Now, I've got work to do."

"When will I hear from you again?" Billy said.

"You get the money lined up. I'll let you know how to get it to me."

Billy put down the phone. His mettle had been tested in many ways in his years as a lawyer and sports agent, but never quite like this.

The right thing and the smart thing weren't necessarily one and the same. *How would he reconcile the two?* He would have to trust his instincts.

"I'll tell you what, Angel. Why don't I come down there and we'll talk a little more about this? I promise that we'll get it worked out to your satisfaction, one way or another."

"There's only one way, and that's with a payoff. One million dollars. You don't need to make the trip yourself, unless you'd like to spend a little time with me. I'm fun."

"I'm sure you are, but I'll pass on that."

"Just get the cash together. Or else Russell Mann is going to be in the national news, and it won't be for signing a new basketball contract. You understand that?"

"I understand."

"I'll call you back tomorrow night. Make the arrangements and be ready. And don't forget, I have proof."

Billy clicked off his phone and rested his chin on it while he thought about what she had said. After a few minutes, he decided to call Russell.

Five rings later, he was preparing to leave a message when the big man answered.

"I just heard from Angel," Billy said. "She wants a million dollars."

"Is that all? Seriously, I ain't giving her jack. She's full of it."

"Maybe so, but she claims she has proof that you were there that night. Maybe it's a video, or a recording of some kind. Maybe another witness. Doesn't sound like she's bluffing."

"I told you I wasn't there, and that's all you need to know. There's no reason to worry about our little Angel anyway." The tone was ominous. "I predict that we'll never hear anything more from her."

"What do you mean, Russell? I'm being put in a very compromised position here, and I don't appreciate it."

"You're my agent and you're just going to have to trust me. That's the way this works. What is it, attorney-client privilege? In the meantime, I'm going on that little vacation you wanted me to take. Leaving tonight with a special friend."

"Where are you going?"

"South. I'll just be gone a couple of days and then we can start working on that fat contract. I think I know what I want to do. Pretty soon there won't be anything left standing in the way. I want you to come down to Florida this weekend and we'll talk. Later, bro."

Billy shook his head again and tossed his phone on the desk in disgust. He was used to managing high-stress situations, being a negotiator, a facilitator, a fixer. Whatever it took to advance the client's interests.

But he'd never had a client like Russell Mann.

CHAPTER THIRTY-SIX

As prostitutes went, Angel was an eye catcher. She could stop traffic with a look and a smile.

With her bold outfits, insatiable cheekbones and frizzy, jet-black hair, she had become a well-known figure in the area near Parramore Avenue and Grand Street. The titillating spectacle of the job, grabbing men's attention, feeding their fantasies, if only for a moment, never got old for Angel. She felt free and powerful walking the streets.

Even with a huge payoff in the works, one that would transform her marginal existence, she couldn't stay away.

The stranger had called an hour earlier, claiming to be a friend of a friend. In a deep voice, he offered her five hundred bucks to go for a ride. It was well above her going rate, and she took it as another sign that she was on the best roll of her life.

When the silver SUV pulled to the curb with the passenger window open, Angel leaned in for a little reassurance. She still needed to be careful.

"I hear you're like heaven, baby," the driver said in that familiar voice, flashing several bills. "I want you to take me there."

She took the cash, looked it over, and discreetly folded it into her white shorts. "Let's go then." The door opened and she slid across the leather seat.

As the SUV headed out of the downtown, Angel began to size up her john. Large black man in a tight navy t-shirt and jeans, built like an NFL linebacker. She liked athletes.

"Why you walking around all alone?" the man said casually, without taking his eyes off the road. "Shouldn't a girl like you be afraid of strangers in this part of town?"

"What can I say? It's the middle of the day, and this is home. I trust you. You said you were a friend of Michael's. How do you know him?"

"We go back a ways. Guess that makes me a friend of yours, too."

"Soon enough, big man. Where we goin'?"

"There's a little place I know right outside town. It's private and we won't be bothered. I want to have you all to myself, no interruptions."

"Five hundred will take you places, but I don't usually go far out of the neighborhood. I have people looking out for me there. You know what I mean?"

The man nodded and headed west on Interstate 4. "You need somebody to keep an eye on you. I'll bet you're a handful," he said.

"Takes two hands, and hang on tight." She giggled.

After several miles, he exited and turned north on a state route. Angel continued to study his face carefully along the way.

Her line of work had given her considerable insight into men, their professional profiles, character, state of mind.

She could find their soft spots, where they were vulnerable. And she could usually sense danger from a distance.

This man looked serious, but not dangerous. Those types tended to be quick and easy transactions.

"You remind me of somebody," Angel said. "What's your name?"

"They call me Reaper."

"That's a strange one. Bet your momma didn't name you that. Do you play ball?"

"Naw," he said, cracking a slight smile. "Me and coaches never got along real well. You like ballplayers?"

"I've known a few. They like *me*."

"I'll bet they do. You ever blow anybody famous?"

"I'm not a girl who likes to blow and tell, but there is one … pro basketball player. Big and tall. He's a shooter, if you know what I mean."

"Let me guess: he plays for the Magic."

A playful expression came over her. "I'm not gonna say."

The SUV turned off the highway and then again, snaking along a two-lane road before slowing at the back of a tract of land that was destined for development. It had yet to be graded and stood as a small piece of wilderness in a rapidly changing landscape.

The driver glanced around as he eased off the pavement onto a dirt path. There were no sights or sounds of activity in the immediate area, so they continued on, stirring up the dust as they went.

"Where in the hell you goin'?" Angel said. "You said you had a place. I thought you meant somewhere we could get out of this heat."

"Almost there."

Finally, they came to a large stand of trees and stopped. Reaper killed the engine and turned toward his passenger. The way he looked at her made Angel uncomfortable. *Could she have been wrong?*

"Here?" she said.

"Here. You can take off those little white shorts now. And I hope you don't mind, but it's going to be a threesome."

Angel gasped as another man suddenly appeared at the rear of the vehicle. He walked along the side and opened her door. With his red bandana, dirty jeans and boots, he looked like a construction worker. Sweat rolled down his bare chest.

"Dexter, meet Angel. Smokin' hot, ain't she?"

She turned back toward the driver with defiance. "What's going on here? I didn't agree to any of this. Who are you? You're not a friend of Michael's."

"No, but I'm a friend of Russell Mann," Reaper said with a toothy grin. "I thought you said you liked ballplayers, especially big, tall basketball players. So why would you want to blackmail a man like Russell? I'm here to tell you, he doesn't appreciate that."

Angel tried to squirm out of her seat, but Dexter shoved her back in. She was trapped between the men, and the growing fear began to register on her face.

Reaper unzipped his pants. "Russell said you were amazing. Show me. Now."

He grabbed a fist full of that frizzy hair and forced her head into his lap as the man behind her began to strip off her shorts.

"Please don't do this," she cried. "I won't call Russell again … I don't want his money. I promise I won't tell the cops or anybody else. I'll leave my story just like it is."

"Why would anybody believe a woman like you, Angel? Tomorrow you'll be saying something different, going to the cops or the press. The only thing I believe is that you're a good whore. And you're about to prove it. Ain't that right, Dex?"

The wiry man smiled but said nothing. He unbuttoned his jeans.

Angel tried to think. She had found herself in so many dicey situations before, but there always seemed to be a way out, an escape route, someone to intervene. This time she felt helpless.

Still, she was determined not to panic.

"You don't know who you're dealing with," she said. "I'm warning you, if you do this, you're going to have more gangbangers coming after you than you can believe. I'm one of them."

"Let me tell you something: I *am* gonna do this," Reaper said. "It's my job. And they *ain't* gonna know what happened to you."

"They'll know. I told them I was waiting for a silver SUV. I'm sure somebody saw us leaving."

"Lots of silver SUVs around. Guess we'll have to see. Only thing I'm worried about right now is getting off."

Angel tried to resist, but it was useless. She was reduced to simply hoping the assault would be quick and painless. And that she'd somehow be free to go afterward.

Sprawled out across the seats, she took the full measure of both men, and then it was over. They were spent.

Now it was time to finish the job.

"I wish we had more time together, but we don't," Reaper said, nodding to his friend.

Dexter yanked Angel out of the car. As she bent down to grab her shorts, her cell phone slipped out of a pocket and into the weeds. When she stood again, they were face to face.

Dexter smiled. He knew what was coming next.

From behind, Reaper pulled a black string tight across Angel's throat. Her eyes bugged and she gagged, her arms flailing wildly before going limp. Reaper finally relaxed his hold and let the body fall to the ground.

"Pretty girl," he said, standing over her. "Did you get that hole dug?"

"Over here, but it's not deep enough. Didn't have time."

The sound of machinery starting up in the distance caused the men to freeze for a moment.

"It'll have to do," Reaper said. "We need to go. Grab some of that brush for cover."

Reaper dragged the body to the makeshift grave. Before rolling it into the hole, he reached down and pulled the folded bills from Angel's pocket. Then in she went, face down at first.

"Let's turn her over," Reaper said. "Least we can do is let Angel be facing heaven."

"Probably won't help," Dexter said as he began to shovel the dirt over her. He worked quickly, sweeping the area with a dead tree branch and then hiding the shallow grave.

The men jumped in the SUV and circled back toward the road. For the time being, Angel Rivera's secret was buried with her.

CHAPTER THIRTY-SEVEN

The rushing waters outside the King mansion created a distinctive sound, soothing yet relentless. It reminded Billy of some of the smaller streams in the Smokies. He couldn't help but stop and listen, again.

The last time he had passed by the fountain, a bronze masterpiece of blue herons grazing in a marsh, he was about to leave Isle of Palms, dazed and confused. A confrontation with Rachel had confirmed his suspicions. She admitted to being with his brother John when he picked up cocaine, a bribe from the mob, while they were on a business trip in Florida. Billy had found a small vial of the powder in her purse upstairs.

It was the beginning of the end. The next day John was dead, and the whole Jarvis Thompson affair spiraled out of control.

Billy stood still, almost overwhelmed by the memories. He wished he could forget so many things.

The heavy oak door of the Mediterranean opened, and Elaine King stood before him. She was a striking woman, tall and lithe, much like her daughter. They had once gotten along well. In fact, Billy had often been a guest in the house.

Now he was just a painful reminder of the family's loss.

"Hello, Billy," Elaine said with a faint smile. "Come in."

The door had barely closed when Bradley King entered from his study. He reached out to shake the agent's hand.

"I didn't expect to see you again this soon," he said. "I was surprised when you called."

"I'm on my way to Florida and thought we could talk. I wanted to do it in person."

"That's fine. We can go outside to the gazebo; it's another nice day on the coast. You want something to drink?"

"No, thanks. I can't stay long."

"Is anything wrong?" Elaine said.

"I'm not sure, to be honest. I just came across some new information and need to know more if possible."

The Kings drew closer to him, wide-eyed. "About *Rachel*?" Elaine said. Billy nodded.

"She apparently has been back in Knoxville, at least a couple of times recently."

Elaine gasped and latched on to her husband's arm. "How do you know?"

"She approached my assistant, Jackson, a while back at his place. Just showed up out of the blue."

"Your *assistant*? Why are we just now hearing about it?"

"I don't have a good answer for that. I just found out myself."

"So where is she?" Bradley said.

Billy took a deep breath. "I don't know that either. I'm sorry."

"So what *do* you know?"

"I know Rachel was asking about me, wanting information. And she put Jackson in a compromising position to get it."

"What did she want to know?"

"He said she was mostly interested in Holly, my relationship with her and when we were going to be together. Holly thought she saw Rachel at a golf tournament in Arizona. I didn't believe her when she first mentioned it, but now I'm not sure. There were some other things, too."

Elaine stumbled over to a chair and sat as Billy gauged the reaction of her husband. "Jackson had a sense that there's more to the story, something we didn't know. And he seemed to think it might involve you, Bradley, that you know the real reason she left Charleston. Rachel led him to believe that."

Elaine turned toward Bradley with an icy glare.

"Me?" Bradley said. "That's ridiculous, Billy. You and I spent two days together in New Orleans and turned over every stone. Did it seem to you that I was hiding anything? Would I have taken you along if that was the case?"

"I'm just looking for answers anywhere I can find them. There's no shortage of questions, or surprises. As I've said many times before, none of this makes sense. Help me understand."

Bradley turned and walked to the large wall of glass at the back of the great room. He stepped through the door and out onto the sprawling deck with Billy trailing close behind. The Atlantic sparkled just beyond the dunes. There wasn't a more breathtaking vantage point on Isle of Palms.

Bradley's eyes darted back and forth. "Billy, why do I feel a need to defend myself here?" he said.

"That's a good question."

"So you've come to tell me my daughter is out there, still alive, but you don't know where. And then you accuse me of, *what*? Causing her disappearance? Being complicit in some sort of scheme? It doesn't make any sense."

"That's what I've been saying."

The men stood face to face. "I don't need this, Billy," King said. "I think you should leave."

"We're going to finish this conversation now. Tell me what was going on the day she left. What made her pack up and disappear? I can't believe it was just a desire to go live with Paul Romano. It was more than that."

The expression on Elaine's face suddenly grew stern. "You're going to tell him, Bradley. There's no reason to hold back now."

Bradley clenched his jaw and steeled himself.

"Rachel was … pregnant," he said. "She had been experiencing some morning sickness and didn't know why. It was confirmed by her doctor."

The news stunned Billy. He cocked his head and looked at the couple in disbelief.

"Pregnant? With *whose* child?"

"She wasn't sure, but she seemed to think it was Paul Romano's," Elaine said. "I tried talking to her about it, but she pushed me away. When she left, she was in a state of confusion. We wouldn't have let her leave if we'd known just how bad it was."

"Why on earth didn't you tell me?"

"She demanded that we keep it a secret. And there's still no certainty. The fact that she went to New Orleans to be with Romano suggests that she had decided the baby wasn't yours."

Billy rubbed his face and tried to make sense of it all.

"So it was *his*? Then why is she stalking *me*? Why seduce Jackson to get information? Why not just come to me? I don't get it."

The Kings each looked as though they'd taken a heavy punch to the gut. There was a long silence, and then Elaine quickly pivoted and disappeared down the hallway. Billy could hear her making her way up the staircase.

"I don't like any of this," he said, turning to Bradley. "What else are you holding back? I deserve to know."

"There's nothing more. What you've told me just makes it more imperative: We have to find Rachel. Now."

"I'm on my way to Florida, but you can be sure I won't let this rest. I don't think anybody can until this is resolved. She may be out there with a child. *My* child."

The big door slammed shut. Bradley watched Billy get in his car and leave the estate. He dropped heavily into a chair, ran his fingers through his silver hair, and stared at the floor.

Elaine was coming back down the stairs, slowly. She turned the corner at the bottom and stopped with a grim expression on her face.

The little girl in her arms cooed softly.

"He has a right to know," Elaine said. "If you don't tell him, I will."

CHAPTER THIRTY-EIGHT

T he agent was almost to Windermere the next morning when his phone rang, snapping him back to attention. The last eighteen hours had been a blur.

Russell was calling from the Miami airport. He and his travel companion were on hold at the gate, waiting for their flight to Orlando, which had been delayed by mechanical problems.

Russell sounded cheerful, almost happy. Strange. Maybe the short vacation had cleared his head, made him forget. His agent certainly hadn't forgotten anything.

"Hopefully won't be much longer getting out of here," he said. "Should have taken a charter."

"What do you want me to do?" Billy said.

"Just wait at the house."

"You don't need me to pick you up? I can head back to the airport and we can go on toward the arena."

"No, my car is there. I have to drop off my friend first. Go on to the house and I'll be there in a few hours. You can use the touchpad on the back door to get in. Twenty-five, twenty-five. It's our little secret."

"Right. Jersey number, twice. Clever."

"You'll have to disarm the alarm in the hallway, too."

"Let me guess. Same number."

"Uh-huh. Already got too many damn passwords and numbers. Gotta keep things simple."

"I don't think you're supposed to make it that simple, Russell. When did you start arming the security system anyway? It's about time but doesn't sound like you."

"Finally started last week. Didn't grow up worrying about shit like that. If somebody wanted in your house in Hunts Point, they just came in. But a man can't be too careful these days. Isn't that what you said?"

"We've got a lot more to talk about. You know I scheduled our meeting with Larry West for late afternoon, four o'clock. We may need to move it back to tomorrow if you can't be there."

"Why?"

"It always helps at this stage of the game when the player is actually in the room and involved and excited. Team officials tend to like that. They're making a major investment. I know you'd rather not, but it's just smart business."

"You can go on without me. I want to get everything out on the table with the Magic, sooner the better. You know the deal. Let's get it done."

"You've worked for this your whole life, and it needs to be done right," Billy said. "Whether you stay in Orlando or not, it'll be one of the blockbuster deals in the league this year. We're still not there yet, but we're getting close. The problem is this other thing that popped up. It's a huge black cloud on the horizon. You haven't forgotten?"

"I told you not to worry about that. I'm clean."

"Believe me, I'm worrying, big time. I'm not sure how to handle it."

"Go grab a shower, man. The one in the back guest room has, like, twenty jets."

"I'll do that and then head back toward town. I want to be close. Let me know where you stand time-wise. If you can get here soon enough, we'll just meet at the Amway Center."

"I'm working on it. Ain't no faster than the airline."

"I'll be waiting to hear."

Billy passed through the Whispering Pines gates and eased down to the end of the cul-de-sac. It was another sunny day in central Florida, but he could feel a storm brewing. He pulled his Escalade around the house and parked in front of the four-car garage.

The mailbox in the breezeway was overflowing, and Billy cleared it before stepping up to the door and letting himself in. Twenty-five, twice.

From time to time, the agent had the run of many of his clients' homes and vacation pads. They treated him like family, always eager to share in their good fortune. After all, he had orchestrated their ascent, sometimes from nowhere, like Russell.

The relationship with the Magic star, however, always felt like an awkward collaboration, some sort of charade. And it was surely going to get more so once the player was back in town and they began to sort through everything.

Could Angel Rivera be telling the truth? If she was, then what? Pay her off and ignore the explosive implications? Negotiate the contract and keep quiet? Or tell the cops what he knows and potentially be left with nothing, except the taint of being Russell Mann's agent? That could have lasting consequences.

Of course, Billy had survived more than one public-relations disaster already. If nothing else, he was a survivor. Maybe that was the common bond with Russell.

He opened the refrigerator and shook his head. Nothing but a few cans of Bud Light and some cheese. He slid out a stool at the counter and sat.

The conversation with Bradley and Elaine King continued to play in his mind, over and over. One narrative bled into the other, and he couldn't be sure where either was leading.

Rachel has a child? Where are they both now?

He could feel the crush again, the weight of circumstances beyond his control. Complications on top of complications. For an agent, nothing was worse than losing control.

Every sound seemed to echo in the spacious kitchen. There was an emptiness about the place. Billy mindlessly scanned his email for a few minutes, then set his phone on the gold-flecked granite and rubbed his eyes. Time for that hot shower.

As he stood, he noticed the stack of mail he'd thrown down on the counter. On top was a bill, a monthly power bill from Orlando Utilities, but not for the Windermere house. The address was in Orlovista. *Orlovista?*

He picked up the bill and studied it for a moment. Maybe it was one of Russell's girlfriends' places. The player had never mentioned it. Then again, he never mentioned much of anything.

Billy checked his watch, grabbed his travel bag, and headed up the staircase.

***

Orlovista was perhaps ten miles to the northeast, not far out of the way, and GPS directed him to the back of a small neighborhood on the edge of town. The wooded lot was overgrown, neglected for the most part, but Billy could tell from the fresh tire tracks in the sandy soil along the driveway that people had been coming and going.

He got out of his Escalade and walked to the porch. The blinds in all the windows were drawn, so he went around back to take a look. There were no parked vehicles, and the modest clapboard house was locked up tight. The property didn't look like anything that might belong to an NBA player.

An old garage stood out back, and Billy approached the side door and twisted the knob. To his surprise, the door cracked and he looked in. He could see a covered vehicle in the shadows and stepped inside. Peeling back the fabric revealed a dusty black sedan, a Ford Taurus with oversize gold rims.

He narrowed his eyes. *Hadn't he seen the car before?*

Suddenly there was a rustling at the garage door. It swung open and two men stepped inside. One was holding a handgun.

"What are you doing here?" said the other, in a booming voice.

Billy raised his hands slightly and tried to stay cool. "Didn't mean to interrupt, gentlemen, but I was looking for Russell. Have you seen him?"

"Russell? Who are you?"

"I'm his agent, Billy Beckett." He extended his hand, but the men didn't move. "Haven't we met?"

"No."

"Well, I couldn't get him at home. Thought he might be here."

The man with the gun glared suspiciously at the tall stranger. "In Orlovista? Why you think that? You way out of your neighborhood, bro. And why you in here looking at this car?"

"No reason. Again, I'm just trying to find Russell."

Billy was surprised the man had not yet pointed the weapon at him. The look in his eyes said he wanted to. The tension was palpable as they all stood there, sizing each other up. After a minute, the agent was waved back toward the door.

"Russell is out of town. I would have thought his agent would know that."

"I've been gone myself. We have meetings scheduled today, and I got in a little early." Billy chuckled. "No need to worry about it. I'll just go on out to Windermere and wait on him. Sorry to bother you."

The men glanced at each other, unsure of whether to let the stranger pass. They finally stepped aside, and Billy strode quickly to his Escalade without looking back.

He started the engine, breathed a sigh of relief, and sped away from the Flophouse.

The man with the gun watched until Billy was out of sight before pulling a phone from his back pocket.

"Russell," he said, "I got a question."

CHAPTER THIRTY-NINE

The Magic GM dug his fingernails into the leather arms of his office chair and grimaced. From across the desk, it was obvious that Larry West was anxious. He wanted to put the negotiations behind him, get the star player's status resolved, one way or another, turn his attention to other important personnel decisions. As an organization, the Magic wanted to move smartly into the offseason.

Now West was being told there was a delay. Russell was not going to make the meeting, and that only complicated the day and raised more doubts. *Was the Orlando brass getting cold feet?*

"I'll be honest with you, Billy," West said, hardly trying to conceal his angst. "I'm beginning to wonder if this is the smartest move for our organization. It's a huge investment, and I'm not getting good vibes right now. The social media chatter hasn't helped, but it rarely does. If I'm uncomfortable with the situation, it's hard to reassure ownership that we're doing the right thing. And if that doesn't change, you may find your client wearing another uniform next season."

SCOTT PRATT

Billy was used to executives hedging, spinning, deflecting. It was standard operating procedure, especially at negotiating time.

"Don't bring more drama to this than already exists, Larry. You guys need Russell — he's your foundation — and I know he's excited about a possible long-term future in Orlando. He wanted to be here today to tell you himself. We can all relate to airline problems, right?"

"Let me be clear. This isn't about whether Russell is sitting here right now. I'd feel better if he was, but we have to look at the big picture for the team. Here's the pressing question: Is it possible for the Magic franchise to improve if we lose our best player? I don't know, but it could happen. I still have to sell our owners on giving Russell this huge contract. They never dreamed we'd be pushing a hundred million dollars, but all these other free agents are playing into the market, raising the stakes. And here we are."

"Everybody is in that boat right now; we all knew it was coming. These are big decisions for teams, men like yourself, and they're always calculated risks to some extent. You know Russell could probably get more out on the open market. There's no bravado in that statement. There's also a lot of truth in saying that he likes Orlando, feels comfortable here. You guys took a chance on him when others didn't, and he appreciates that."

"You're not suggesting loyalty will play a major role in this, are you?"

Both men smiled knowingly. "Maybe not a major role," Billy said. "But it is a factor."

"In some ways, this is a roll of the dice for the franchise. We're not the richest guys in this game, but we're still trying to win a championship. We have to be creative with the cap. And like I told you the last time you were sitting here, there are some legitimate character issues with Russell. If those turn into legal issues, my ass is on the line. It would tarnish the whole franchise. I have enough problems without worrying about that."

"I appreciate your position, and I've expressed your concerns to Russell. If we do reach agreement on a new contract, he has assured me that there will be no distractions to the team because of bad behavior on his part. He'll be a solid citizen. And he'll give you everything he's got on the court, like he always has. Maybe the next time the playoffs roll around, it'll be a different story."

Billy let the thought linger for effect. "Let's be honest. You're not going to get there without him."

"What else are you going to say?" West said, standing abruptly and looking at his watch. "I don't know if you've made me feel any better about this, Billy, but under the circumstances I'll give you credit for trying. I'm interested to see if we can get a deal done, or if your client really wants to go out and test the open market. There are others out there. The ball is in his hands, so to speak. Let's talk again tomorrow."

***

Billy left the arena and walked briskly toward the parking area. He got into his Escalade and checked his phone, which had vibrated a few times while he spoke with West.

There was a sinking feeling as he tapped the most recent missed call. "What's up, Dad?"

"Not me, unfortunately," came the weak reply. "I'm lying here in the hospital."

"What happened?"

"I just took a turn for the worse at work today. Just ran out of gas. The doctors are trying to figure out where we are and the best approach moving forward."

"Best approach?"

"Best option. Surgery, radiation, chemo ... they're all possibilities. Something has to happen soon."

"*Soon?* How soon?"

"We need to get on this. Hopefully it's not too far along, but they say the prognosis isn't great no matter what. They're just being honest with me; I told them not to hold back. I'm afraid I'm learning a lot more than I wanted to know about this disease."

"Tell me. Please."

"They said it's the most common type, but still pretty uncommon as cancer goes. Pleural mesothelioma. Had to be exposure to asbestos, and it could have been building inside me for twenty or thirty years. Who knows? That's the problem: it's usually diagnosed at a late stage, so recovery is tougher. Only about forty percent make it longer than a year."

The tears were filling Billy's eyes again and his voice quavered. "You know I'm in Florida," he said. "I told you I'd always be there for you, no matter what, and I'm not. I feel terrible."

"There's nothing you can do, son. Worrying doesn't help. You have to keep living your life, doing your job, and let me fight this as best I can."

"I shouldn't be hearing about this on the phone."

"I know, and I'm sorry for that. I just didn't want you to be surprised when you got home. I'm not exactly sure what my situation will be then … we're waiting to see the latest test results. It was better for us to talk now."

"I'm on my way, Dad. I'll be on the next flight out."

"Billy, don't …"

Billy dropped his phone and rubbed his face. He needed a minute to collect himself.

Finally, he got out of the car and walked back toward the Magic executive offices. There would be no meeting tomorrow either.

CHAPTER FORTY

T y Nelson had envisioned the scene from the start.
If he made it to the final night of The Songmasters,
he was going to pull out his flashiest guitar, sing one
of his favorite songs, and blow everybody away. And now
here he was, standing on stage in L.A. in all black, the
movie star looks, the koa six-string with the pearl inlay
at his side, just like in Claire's picture. Win or lose, he
had made his mark. He had *arrived*.

The cover of *She Wouldn't Be Gone*, an old Blake
Shelton hit about a foolish man chasing after lost love,
had been true to Ty's country roots. The fans loved it.
The song also set him apart from the three other finalists — Lori, the Kenny Chesney backup singer who was
mesmerizing with a Linda Ronstadt classic; Amy, the
chiseled blonde teenager who revved up the place with a
powerful Pink cover; and Timothy, the beefy bartender
from New York who gamely belted out *Whipping Post* by
the Allman Brothers.

Was it good enough? Everyone in the building and
a national television audience was about to find out. A
combination of instant voting by telephone, Internet and
text would determine the champion.

Ty's entourage was feeling the effects of four tense days in town. His parents and sister had squirmed in their seats throughout his performance. It was the last of the competition; now the excruciating wait. Viewers had ten minutes to weigh in.

Trying to burn nervous energy, Claire was pacing along the rear of the hall and could only stand and watch as the finalists were called back to the stage. They linked arms next to hostess Frannie Townsend and awaited their fate.

Townsend, a leggy Brit who stood more than six feet tall in her high heels, was a towering presence on stage. She beamed with that perfect smile before going down the line with her microphone for a short conversation with each of the artists.

Ty was the last to answer the simple question: *What have you learned about yourself over the last month?* He didn't hesitate.

"I've learned about making lasting relationships," he said. "Everyone here has incredible talent, but the relationships are what this business is all about. I want to thank everyone at The Songmasters, all my fans in Nashville, and a few really special people out there in the audience. We've come a long way together. I love you."

His family was almost in tears. Claire, still standing in the back, found herself fighting to catch her breath as she moved to join the others. The emotion had consumed them all.

The countdown was about to begin. The final balloting was handed to the hostess.

First out was Timothy, the bartender. Then Amy, the relative youngster in the group. They stepped aside knowing the exposure had already guaranteed national celebrity and successful tours in the coming months.

Many observers had figured all along that Lori Green would be center stage at the finish. She was a seasoned pro with a distinctive sound and polished look, perfect for a competition like this one. But in a short time Ty had created an exciting brand of his own, and that couldn't be discounted.

So the Nashville stars remained. They stood together, shining brightly, holding hands, pondering this career-altering moment. The audience rose as one, roared again, and then suddenly grew quiet.

Frannie Townsend ratcheted up the drama a final time: "And the winner of The Songmasters, who will receive a cash prize of $250,000 and a recording contract with Sterling Records, is …"

***

The line echoed through his head as Ty rolled over in bed and squinted at the clock. Six a.m.

The redhead nestled close, rubbing her breasts on his back, and giggled. "You okay? Sounded like you were whimpering in your sleep."

"I dreamed I won, or was about to," he said, turning toward her. "I'm still shaking. Crazy."

"It's not crazy, but we're not quite there yet. Tonight. You'll be great."

Claire took his face gently in her hands and kissed him.

"You can quit shaking now," she said. "I told you I wasn't going to do this again. And here I am, in your suite, beside you in bed, at six in the morning. I should be asleep down the hall. Remember, you insisted."

"No complaints, ma'am. I appreciate you tucking me in properly, keeping my confidence level high. I needed that."

"I know we've already been through it, but I have to say it again: I'm your agent and should know better."

Ty smiled like an experienced lover who knew exactly what he was doing. "It's the music. You remember Greek mythology? The muses?"

"What?"

"When I was young, I always noticed how the ladies moved toward the musicians without even thinking. They really liked the athletes, but they *loved* the musicians, the muses. The emotional connection is stronger. Wouldn't you agree?"

"I might right this moment, but I have to tell you, we love all kinds of players at Premier. I guess the fact that you're our first client with a guitar makes you a special muse." She rubbed his biceps. "Do you feel special?"

"Come here, ma'am, and let me show you again."

"Quit calling me ma'am, country boy." Claire moved away playfully and flipped on the television. "Sorry, but I need to get back to my room, and you need to get up and moving. This is *your* day. Just remember, even if you don't win tonight — and I know it's hard to imagine — you're already a star to millions of people. They love you and want to see more. I can't wait to see where your career goes from here."

With that, she picked up her dress from the floor and eased toward the bathroom. Before she reached the door, she stopped to check her phone on the dresser.

There was a text message from Billy. *Call me when you can.* She walked into the bathroom and closed the door behind her, then flipped on the fan.

"I just saw your text," she said. "I forgot to turn the ringer back on last night. What's going on?"

"I'm back in Knoxville," Billy said.

"I thought you were going to stay in Florida for a few days."

"I flew home last night. Dad isn't doing well."

Claire put down the toilet lid and took a seat. "What do you mean?"

"He's in the hospital … I just left there. I'm afraid this cancer is killing him."

"So it's mesothelioma?"

"It looks that way. We'll know more soon."

From thousands of miles away, Claire could feel Billy's pain. The connection between them always got stronger in crisis. But for once, she didn't know what to say to make things better.

"I just wanted you to be aware that my plans had changed," he said. "Everything is up in the air for the moment. Russell got stuck in Miami and couldn't make the meeting with Larry West yesterday, and we were going to get together today. Then Dad called. He doesn't think he has much time left and is talking crazy."

"You just see to your father and don't worry about anything with Russell. I understand you think it's important to get his contract nailed down ASAP, but he's in a strong position. That's going to work out for the best, regardless. You'll make sure of it."

Billy chuckled nervously. "You think so?"

"You don't?"

"I wasn't getting positive vibes in Orlando. I'm not getting positive vibes anywhere right now."

"You don't sound very good, Billy. What can I do to help? I can come home if you need me."

"Don't be ridiculous. The big night with Ty is almost here. That's important for everybody. I'll figure this out. I guess I just wanted to hear your voice."

There was a long pause. "Give Ty my best," he said. "We'll talk again after the show."

CHAPTER FORTY-ONE

A sense of dread hung over Franklin Beckett, but he was strong enough to go home to Sevierville.

The next move in his treatment had yet to be determined. Doctors were prepared to follow up aggressively if X-rays revealed that the fluid buildup in his lungs had returned. There would be more tests for cancer cells. PET scans and CT scans, looking for any suspicious masses, would follow.

If worse came to worst, a surgeon would schedule a biopsy of fluid and tissue samples to determine the clinical staging, how far the disease had advanced. By then a battery of other doctors — pulmonologist, radiologist, pathologist, oncologist — would also be on the case.

Franklin said he didn't want to think about any of it anymore. For one of the few times in his life, he felt powerless. He closed his eyes and pushed back in the old recliner in his den. Within moments, he was starting to drift.

Billy sat on the couch, just a few feet away and studied his father's face. It seemed that Franklin had aged years in just the last few weeks. He was increasingly tired and short of breath.

Where would they be a month from now? Or six months? Billy was afraid to ask.

"Son, how about turning on the television or something that makes noise," Franklin said. "The silence in here is deafening."

Billy grabbed the remote and started to look for an NBA playoff game. His father loved basketball. Any kind of game would be a welcome distraction.

Suddenly, it dawned on him. He'd completely forgotten about The Songmasters. He quickly flipped the channel. There was Ty Nelson's smiling face on the screen. He was standing on stage, holding hands with a brunette in a sparkly blue dress. The competition had apparently boiled down to just the two of them, and it was almost over.

The bubbly hostess was holding a card and beaming. The audience held its collective breath. Billy leaned forward and stared intently.

"And the winner of The Songmasters, who will receive a cash prize of $250,000 and a recording contract with Sterling Records, is … Lori Green!"

Ty gave the champion a big hug and stepped away as the music blared and a blizzard of confetti and balloons began to rain down from above.

Billy slumped back into the cushion. For a moment, he had a new reason to be disappointed. "Damn," he said, and flipped over to ESPN.

"What is it?" Franklin said groggily.

"Nothing. Just another tough loss. We'll go back to basketball. Do you need anything?"

"Something cold to drink would be good. Water, please."

Billy walked into the kitchen and pulled a plastic bottle out of the refrigerator. The steps seemed so familiar, so mindless, he could have done it blindfolded. He turned and sat down again next to his father, who caught a brief second wind after a sip or two from the bottle.

"Your mother," Franklin said. "Do you still think much about her?"

The words took Billy by surprise. "All the time."

"She was a beautiful lady, always there for her family, for you boys."

Billy bit his lip. He and his father had not spoken much about Anna's death in recent years, but it was never far from Billy's mind. The car accident, with his hand on the wheel, had changed all of their lives. The guilt never went away, and his father tried not to make things worse.

"I never could have imagined going on in this life without her, or your brother," Franklin said. "John didn't deserve to die like that. You and me, we didn't deserve it either."

There was a long pause. "I don't want to leave you alone, son."

Billy couldn't muster a response without breaking down, so he didn't try. He rubbed his father's shoulder as he tried to catch his breath.

Franklin soon returned to his dream world, and Billy sat back and stared at the television screen. The Greek Freak was driving for another easy basket. The Bucks were going to be hard to beat.

The phone rang in Billy's pocket, and he quickly got up and walked down the hallway.

"Hey," he said. "I saw the end. Looked like Ty did everything but win."

Claire hid her disappointment well. She sounded more like the discriminating agent than the passionate woman who woke up in Ty Nelson's bed that morning.

"He was incredible, but you can't take anything away from Lori Green," she said. "We all thought coming into this thing that she was the favorite, and she was brilliant tonight. Two bright Nashville stars on the rise. Could have gone either way."

"It was still a great thing for Ty, for you, for us. I look forward to working with him, seeing how far this can go. His popularity is through the roof right now, but we need to have a bigger plan ready."

"Really? I hadn't thought of that."

The dripping sarcasm made Billy realize his mistake. Claire always had a plan. In some ways, he was along for the ride on this one anyway.

"Okay, Claire, just keep me posted. I'm assuming there will be some others coming along, too, in the near future. You promised me, remember?"

"Count on it. How's your father?"

Billy glanced back into the den. "He's resting. This is a really tough stretch, and I don't know where we're headed. He just brought up my mother, which he doesn't do very often when we're together. It means he's thinking the end is near."

"Your dad is a tough guy," Claire said, "and so are you."

"Unfortunately, we've all had to toughen up over the last couple of years. The hits just don't seem to let up."

"That's the truth. We should all be used to heartache at this point, if a person ever gets used to it. Is there anything I can do?"

"No. Thanks."

"I need to go now, but I'll be back late tomorrow. I'll call when I get home."

"Safe travels, Claire. Tell Ty he's a champ regardless. We're all really proud."

Billy stuck the phone back in his pocket and walked toward his father, who despite the raspy breathing appeared to be at peace in his favorite chair with Lucy wedged beside him. So many battles had yet to be fought.

CHAPTER FORTY-TWO

Reaper was waiting when the big man pulled around the house and walked inside. The look of aggravation on Russell's face was unmistakable as he slammed the door behind him. He dumped his shoulder bag in the middle of the kitchen floor.

"Damn airline," he said. "I should have just stayed down in the Caribbean; had everything I wanted. Nice cabana, hot little woman. I ain't got time to waste sitting around in airports. Too much goin' on."

He grabbed a beer from the refrigerator and shook his head. "So Billy's been out at the Flophouse?"

"He saw T-Bone's car," Reaper said. "Not sure what else, but he got a good look at the place. Don't know if he realized anything."

"What did he say?"

"Nothing. He played it cool, just said he was looking for you. How did he know?"

Russell drummed his fingers on the counter and gazed down at the stack of mail with the power bill on top. He picked it up and pursed his lips.

"I can't afford to have him doing anything but getting this deal worked out. We're so damn close. He can't be distracted by things that don't matter. Why would he go to Orlovista?"

Reaper shook his head. "Where is he now?"

"Went back to Tennessee. Sent me a text saying his father was sick and he had to go. Just left his car at the airport and flew home. I don't know how soon he'll be back, or what he's gonna say about this when I see him again."

"Seems like he wouldn't wanna know much about it. He's got a lot at stake."

"Yeah, but he's a different kind of dude. Always preaching to do the right thing, even if it's wrong. He's different than most agents I know of. I should have gotten rid of him a while back."

"Still, he don't wanna ruin a deal like this. Could cost him millions, right?"

"Could. But we're not gonna let that happen. He's on board whether he likes it or not. We'll have to see how the ride ends for him."

"Looks to me like there's trouble everywhere, Russell. Who knows what's coming down the road? You worried?"

"You ever seen me worried?"

Reaper shook his head and smiled. "Not really. Seen times where you shoulda been. This is one of those."

"If I spent time worrying, I never would have gotten out of Hunts Point. Never would have been a millionaire."

"How to keep you shining. That's the question. What now?"

Russell took a deep breath and walked to the windows. There was an air of anticipation; something game-changing was about to happen. It was like being on the court in a tight game, crowd roaring, emotions running high. He could feel it coming.

For a fleeting moment, Russell's mind skipped back to his youth, and the corrupt smile naturally appeared. It was a sign: he still enjoyed the chase and was confident he could win.

"First thing is get that car out of the shed, make it disappear," he said. "Should have done that already. We might need to do something with the house, too, give it a good sweep and move on. It's in T-Bone's name, and I don't want any ties to me. T-Bone needs to be a ghost for all time."

"Like Angel?"

Russell smiled again. "Gone, gone, gone. Billy's gonna be waiting a long time for that call. You enjoyed meeting her, didn't you, Reaper?"

"For a few minutes. That's all it took."

"No chance of her turning up?"

"Don't worry. Her little secret is buried deep."

"Better be. You go on now and see about the house and car. And let me know if there's any more trouble. I'll make it worth your while, like always. I'm counting on you, Reaper."

***

The secret was not buried deep enough.

Angel's gang had tracked her cell phone signal when she didn't return to Parramore and found the shallow grave. They spent the last couple of days checking around, trying to put the pieces together. *Who was responsible?*

Witnesses in the neighborhood confirmed that Angel had left with a man in a silver SUV. But he was no friend of Michael Forney, who actually had departed Florida weeks before. *So what was the connection?*

Finally, the real break. Another prostitute came forward and said Angel confided that she had seen Russell Mann the night of the double murder in Parramore. Just sitting there in the back of the car, smiling.

Angel was ecstatic, the woman said, about cashing in on what she knew. Didn't want to share the information, or the money, with anyone else. If she was afraid, she didn't show it.

Now the gang had her lifeless body and a clearer picture of what happened: Russell had arranged to have her silenced, once and for all. They had the leverage. And there was more: A piece of paper with a phone number scribbled on it was found in a pocket of Angel's shorts.

The woman who answered made it sound important: "Premier Sports and Entertainment."

***

"One more thing," Reaper said. "You gonna tighten the screws on your agent?"

Russell didn't hesitate. "I'm waiting to see. Everything needs to come together soon if Billy wants to keep from drowning in his own mess. He doesn't want you going down to Fort Lauderdale to visit his friend Holly, now does he? That's always possible. He'd have to think about that."

Both men smiled. "Could have other things going against him, too," Reaper said. "Maybe players show up who were paid in college. For agents, that's like poison."

"But that's a slow burn. You never know what's out there that could do a man harm."

Reaper looked dead serious now. "We could always drive around the airport parking lot, find his car, do a little wiring job. I learned that in the military. You'd have to get a new agent, but you wouldn't have to worry about some other things."

"There's no reason for that. Not yet. But things could change in a hurry. We need to be ready."

CHAPTER FORTY-THREE

Billy returned to Florida three days later. By the time he arrived in Windermere, he had decided to throw it all out there on the table with Russell and was bracing for the blowback.

The agent wouldn't knowingly help cover up a murder — maybe several murders. His conscience, his sense of decency, wouldn't let him perpetuate this bizarre reign of terror, even if it meant losing the most lucrative deal he'd ever negotiated.

Or would it?

Billy expected Russell to be perfectly honest, for once. Unless he was sure, there would be no need to meet again with Lawrence West. They would cut ties and he would move on, let the legal process take its course. The star forward would be someone else's problem. That was the plan.

Russell was sitting outside in the grass next to the koi pond when Billy eased up the driveway. His eyes were closed and his long legs folded in some sort of yoga pose that ran contrary to his whole paranoid persona. Russell was normally about as Zen as a day trader.

Billy stopped his car, stepped outside, and slowly made his way along the flagstone walkway. He could hear the flowing water of the fountain babbling quietly as he approached Russell, who didn't move or even seem to notice. That was strange, too. The player was always keenly aware of his surroundings, quick to establish his turf.

"You okay?" Billy said.

Russell opened his eyes but betrayed no emotion. "How's your father?" he said.

The question caught Billy off guard, almost as much as the setting outside the front door of the house. Russell had never asked about the agent's family. Ever.

"He's pretty sick. Cancer, it looks like."

"Really sorry, man. Do you want to sit? We can talk here."

Billy glanced around, as if waiting for someone to intervene, snap Russell back to reality.

"In the grass? Are you sure you're okay? You're not high on something, are you?"

There was only a small shake of the head. Billy gathered himself and sat down.

"You know growing up, I never imagined a place like this," Russell said. "Big house in Florida with a pool and a fish pond. Fancy cars. All mine. I wish my momma could see it."

The soft tone of this hardened kid from the ghetto was disarming. Billy didn't dare interrupt.

"She did her best." Russell rubbed his face and was struggling with his emotions. "She didn't have much of a chance. She had to fight to stay alive, and you see where that got her. There was nothing I could do to help. Nothing I can do now."

"Do you ever talk to her in prison?"

"No. Wouldn't know where to start."

"She'd be proud that you got out of the projects, made something of yourself. That's what she'd tell you. I'm sure she's proud."

Billy suddenly found himself drawn in, conflicted, trying to muster compassion for someone who had seen the worst violence imaginable. Russell was a victim, too.

"You could have been killed in the streets," Billy said, "but here you are. It's a remarkable story that shows your toughness and grit. I've said it many times before … you're a survivor."

Russell took a deep breath. "Basketball has meant everything to me; it was my ticket out of hell. I have to give you credit, Billy. Even in junior college, no one else wanted me or believed in me like you. You know, I might have left Mississippi and gone back to the Bronx. I'd probably be dead by now. I damn sure wouldn't be *here* if it wasn't for you."

He turned and looked Billy in the eye, in a way the agent had never experienced. It almost seemed that the mentoring, the hectoring, the constant back and forth of the last several years had registered at some level.

There was a bond between them, however fleeting, and it would be put to the test today.

"Do you wish you'd never stopped at that little shit-hole college?" Russell asked. "Do you wish you'd never met me?"

"I don't know how to answer that, Russell. It's been an adventure, but we need to talk about what's going on *now*. I need some answers before we can move forward."

That was all it took. Suddenly Russell stiffened and assumed a defensive posture. His personality had changed again. No more Zen.

"Inside," he said sternly, and they both rose to their feet.

The men walked through the house to the kitchen, and Russell pulled out two chairs at the breakfast nook. There was a holstered handgun and box of ammunition on the counter nearby.

"You going shooting?" Billy said.

"Maybe. Sometimes it makes me feel better, just holding a gun in my hand. Want something to drink?"

"No, we just need to talk. So many things have been going on lately that I don't know where to start."

"Go ahead."

"First, I stopped by the house in Orlovista. I'm sure your friends told you."

Russell nodded. "What were you looking for?"

"Nothing really. I never knew you had that property and stopped to take a look on my way back to Orlando. Didn't strike me as something you'd want or need. What is it?"

"Just needed a place for T-Bone to hang out. He's close there but not too close, if you know what I mean."

"I saw the car in the garage; it's his, isn't it? Didn't look like it had been out in a while. Where is he?"

"He went back to the city. Needed to take care of some family things at home."

"Seems like a lot of people have been disappearing lately. I haven't heard anything more from Angel either, and that's strange considering our last conversation.

She was all ready to take you to the cleaners. And now, nothing."

"I told you not to worry."

Billy's eyes narrowed. "Is she dead?"

Russell rubbed his chin and walked to the refrigerator.

"Why would you ask me that?"

"I'm just trying to understand what's going on here, Russell. None of it looks good from my position. A hooker claims to have seen you in the back of a car just before two of her friends were killed. She tries to extort money, and now she's missing. Your best friend's car is stashed away in an old shed several miles from here, and he's missing, too. That doesn't take into account another friend who was shot in the head a few hours after having drinks with you. Is this all coincidence?"

Russell didn't answer.

"I know these people are off the radar for the most part. I mean, who's going to miss them? Right?"

"What are you saying, Billy? That I'm a murderer?"

"I'm saying that if you're connected in any way, we're finished. I'm out. You're going to have to fight this battle on your own. I can't represent you any longer."

Russell leaned on the counter and smiled. He began fidgeting with the holstered gun, which made Billy nervous.

"So you don't believe in me anymore?"

"I want to, but I'm not stupid or blind. You know that. It's all going to come out eventually. Always does."

"You got a lot of money riding on me. It'd be foolish to piss it away for no good reason. We need to get this done, get past all this."

"You don't seem to understand, Russell. If things go bad, you're not going to be playing basketball. You're going to be in prison. For a long time."

Russell casually unsnapped the holster and pulled out the silver gun. It shined in the sunlight that was flooding through the kitchen windows.

"I don't think *you* understand. You and me are a team, and it's game seven. We're going to play this out, all the way to the final horn. There's no other choice."

"So you expect me to go through these contract negotiations like nothing has happened? Just work for my client, cash in, and be happy about it?"

"Exactly."

"You have to know me better than that."

"I know you care about other people, like your friend Holly. You'll do the smart thing. No one cares about poor brothers from New York City, a hooker from downtown. Let it blow over."

"So you're threatening me now?"

Russell snapped the gun back in the holster and stared Billy in the eye again.

"I'm going to make a decision soon," he said. "It's big for both of us. Let's move on. Starting now."

CHAPTER FORTY-FOUR

Jackson Warner had been miserable for weeks, if not months, and his life was spiraling out of control.

He leaned on the bar and tried to make sense of it all. One day he was immersed in his dream job, the only job he ever wanted. The next day he was moving to the West Coast to start anew.

There was no excuse, other than to say that he was foolish and had fallen prey to the oldest temptation on the planet. *He should have been smarter.* Maybe they could engrave that on his headstone.

Jackson threw back the shot glass and gazed out the window. The red car was still there, parked across the street.

"I'm not much of a whiskey drinker," he said to the bartender, a rail-thin woman named Louise with gray hair and a face etched with deep lines. She looked like she had been standing there as long as the building itself. "Let me have a beer, one of the local brews. You pick."

The attorney's nimble mind was restless. His SUV was packed to the brim for the long haul to Seattle and that fresh start. But he had gotten off track right out of Knoxville, dipped south to the Gulf of Mexico.

After nine hours on the road, he was actually farther away than when he started.

In other ways, he was closer than ever to his destination.

Louise plopped down a frosted mug of brown ale on the bar. "They call this one Turbodog," she said. "Damned if I know why. Better be careful about mixing it with whiskey. You know what they say — beer before whiskey, mighty risky. You driving?"

He nodded and sipped the beer.

Jackson was approaching thirty but still had a boyish quality about him. The rosy cheeks and wispy, strawberry blonde hair made him appear closer to twenty. The bartender had even joked about carding him when he first sat down on a stool, as if that were ever a concern in New Orleans.

"You never been in here before, have you?" she asked. "Where you from?"

"Tennessee. Up in the eastern part, near the Smokies."

"I almost guessed that, the way you talk. You're pretty far from home."

He smiled wistfully. "Getting farther, too. Pretty soon I'll be too far to go back."

Jackson had stopped in the French Quarter, near where Rachel King allegedly used to hang out. The odds of tracking her down were long, but he had been showing her picture on his phone — one that Billy had once sent him — to business owners in the area earlier that afternoon.

When he ducked into the bar and flashed it in front of Louise's face, she lit up. Said the woman came in occasionally, either lived nearby or knew someone who did. Drove the red car across the street.

"Hope she's not your wife or girlfriend," Louise said. "I've seen her with a few men. Always seemed like a strange mix to me. She's different."

"No, she's not mine. Just somebody I need to find."

Jackson took another sip from his pint glass and gazed across the street again. The buzz was starting to take hold.

"Let me ask you something, Louise. Why do you think a woman who has everything would want to tear down a poor guy who's just going about his business? Is there sport in that?"

Louise stopped wiping the bar, cocked her head, and tried to size up her only customer. There was an innocence about him, and he sounded sincere. He was unlike most of the rough-cut men who stopped by to drink in the middle of the afternoon.

"You said your name is Jack, right? Let me tell you, Jack, from where I stand there's a lot more damage being done in this world by men. But I don't know in your case. If we're talking about the woman who drives that red car, she looks like somebody who has broken a few hearts. Would yours be one of those?"

"Maybe. I'm not sure it was a matter of heart."

"Well, I wouldn't bother chasing after her. You look like a young man who can find love somewhere else. As the resident expert on spirits and those who come to the Big Easy to cut loose, I've noticed that Tennessee men seem to have a way about them, a certain charm. And I can tell you're a smart one. If I was a lot younger …"

Jackson chuckled for a second and took another swallow of his beer.

"Have you ever disappointed somebody to the point that you just felt sick all the time?" he said. "Like there's no escape, no way to ever make things right?"

"Oh, I've been there. You don't end up running a bar for thirty years without some major heartbreak along the way. But it usually cuts both ways."

"How deep does it cut? That's the question. Can you ever recover?"

"You're starting to lose me, son. Maybe you should go somewhere, get a room, rest a while. When you wake up, you'll feel better."

"I doubt that, Louise, but thanks for the conversation. What do I owe you?"

As he stood at the bar, Jackson noticed the taillights outside. The red car was about to pull into traffic.

He threw down a twenty and hurried out the door.

CHAPTER FORTY-FIVE

By the time he was behind the wheel, Jackson was able to catch only a glimpse of the Mercedes coupe as it turned right on Toulouse Street toward the riverfront.

He took a deep breath, tried to steady himself. The tires squealed and the SUV began to weave through traffic, which was unusually light at this hour in the French Quarter.

After three blocks, he had the car in his sights. Cardinal red C300 with Louisiana dealer tags. Not the kind of car someone would normally drive if they were trying to keep a low profile. Rachel was not a low-profile kind of woman.

The images began to scroll through Jackson's mind — that seductive smile, the athletic build, the soft caress on his cheek. She was a charmer, and she was all his for the taking, at least in that moment. Bad as he felt later, he couldn't help but wonder if he'd do it all over again. She was *that* irresistible.

Jackson pulled alongside at the traffic light and stared across. The angle and dark tinting of the glass made it difficult to distinguish the driver, but he could tell it was a woman with shoulder-length hair and sun-glasses. He rolled down his window and waved franti-cally to get her attention.

The light turned green and she sped away.

Jackson pulled behind her and continued his pursuit until traffic stopped again, near Toulouse Station. He was sure now, and his heart began to race. Rachel King.

She turned right onto Decatur Street and ran south along the Mississippi River. Jackson stayed right on her tail. One missed light and he might never see her again.

Rachel seemed to realize after several blocks that she could not escape, so she slowly continued on, crossing under the Pontchartrain Expressway before finally stop-ping at Lafayette Cemetery.

When she pulled into a parking area, Jackson was right beside her. He quickly jumped out and approached her door. Rachel rolled down the window. She stared at him blankly.

"What are you doing here?" she said.

"I was going to ask you the same thing. You know a lot of people are looking for you, and I'm one of them."

"Why, Jackson?"

"How can you ask me that? You ruined my career, my whole relationship with Billy. You ruined my life."

"I didn't force you into anything. I just wanted some help and you gave it to me. I gave you something in return."

"Simple as that? I don't think some other people, like your parents or Billy, will see it that way. There are a lot of questions."

"Where is Billy? Is he here?"

"I haven't seen him; he's not going to have anything more to do with me, thanks to you. But wherever he is, I'm sure he's trying to figure out what you're up to. Have you just been hiding out in New Orleans? I don't know how you get away with it."

"You don't understand."

"You're damn right. I don't understand anything about this, how I got caught up in it. Why did you leave Tennessee to begin with? What do you want from Billy?"

Rachel looked around and shook her head. "Get in and let me show you."

PART THREE

CHAPTER FORTY-SIX

Billy stared at the text message for several seconds after it pinged in.

Mind made up. Les party.

Billy dropped his phone on the desk and took a deep breath. *Party?* The NBA hadn't even crowned its newest champion yet. There was still a ways to go before the wave of free agents would begin to make their intentions known, much less sign new contracts and celebrate. Most wanted to be sure they had weighed every offer, tested their position in the market.

Russell, apparently, had already decided.

Billy leaned back in his chair and tapped out a response. *Too early. Still a lot up in the air.* His phone rang before he could put it down.

"I want you to get ready for a big announcement," Russell said.

"What kind of announcement?"

"I'm going to stay in Orlando. I've thought about it, and everything I need is here. Let's keep it going. I want you to come back down and get it done."

"Russell…"

"I talked to some people about a fan appreciation thing at Hocus Pocus. They like the idea. I'm the best player on the team, the leader, and the fans will be fired up. It's a big deal that I'm staying."

"That could be true at some point," Billy said, "but now isn't the time. We haven't even settled on terms with the Magic, and there may be a better deal out there. We're talking huge money and need to explore all options. It's still a fluid situation, in more ways than one. I'm juggling."

Russell was insistent. "I don't care what else there is. You're my agent, I've made up my mind, and I want this done. We've talked about the dollars. Make it happen with the Magic. Use *your* magic."

The line went dead and Billy pursed his lips. Russell was beyond his control now; he was testing the agent's conscience and resolve. It was time to have a talk with Claire.

He stood and eased to the door of his office, the sense of dread growing. The place was quiet, but he knew Claire was working on something down the hall. She had been busy since returning from Los Angeles.

Billy knocked gently on her door and she invited him in. "What's up?"

"Sorry to bother you," he said, "but we haven't had much time to talk lately. Looks like you've got a lot going on."

"The Ty Nelson tour is taking shape and I've been covered up. It's amazing how much publicity those music shows can generate. I've got people calling me from all over, wanting to see what it would take to book Ty. We're lining up some of the other musicians he wants to form the band. They're going to open the tour in Florida, and I'm going down there for the first couple of stops, just to make sure we get off to a good start."

"I'm sure it'll be great."

"I've also been communicating back and forth with some other acts that may want to get involved with us. It's a little crazy getting started, but that's a good problem, right?"

"A very good problem. Sorry to be a distraction, but I've been meaning to talk to you about something else for a while. I don't think it can wait any longer. It's Russell, and it's not a good problem."

Claire furrowed her brow. "I'm afraid to ask," she said, closing her laptop. "Let's hear it."

"Well, I just spoke with him and he wants to throw a big party to announce he's staying with the Magic, some fan appreciation thing."

"Now? It's not time for that."

"That's what I told him. But he says he's already made up his mind and wants to let everybody in Orlando know. This *is* Russell Mann we're talking about."

"I don't understand. Doesn't he realize these big contracts take time to negotiate? We've got millions of dollars on the line here. It's a process, and he surely wants to get the best deal. He can't sign officially until the first week of July anyway. I'm sure you've explained all this."

Billy shook his head and gazed out the window. "He knows. There's more to it."

"Oh, boy. Tell me."

"I'm not sure exactly how to put it, but I think Russell may be involved in … criminality."

"*Criminality?* Like what?"

"Murder. Murders."

Claire shot straight up. "Holy shit, Billy. You can't be serious. When? Where?"

"There's reason to believe he and some others have been responsible for the deaths or disappearances of at least three people, and maybe more, in the Orlando area. Street people, just within the last few weeks. Let me be clear, though. I'm not completely sure."

"You're not sure? Explain that to me."

Billy laid out the details as best he knew them. Blue Warren. The men in the car with Angel. Maybe her, too.

"Let's say for the moment that it's possible Russell wasn't directly involved. He knows the people who were."

"Either way, we can't just let that lie without doing something. *Can we?*"

Claire's icy blue eyes were piercing. Billy squirmed in his seat. He had always thought he could manage his way through any adversity, but this was a new level of jeopardy.

"There are all kinds of implications, obviously," he said. "Not the least of which are our reputation and the future of our business."

"We can't be a party to this."

"I told Russell that the other day when we talked at his house — that we're finished if all this sticks, and he'll be going to prison anyway. Things went from strange to dark."

"How so?"

"He was fidgeting with a gun in the kitchen. I don't know if it was even loaded or what was going through his mind, but he pointed out that we're a team and we're going to play this out. It was scary, even by Russell's standards."

"Maybe it's time to go to the police."

"I'm not quite there yet. There may still be some wiggle room. I need to be sure, considering what's at stake."

"Wiggle room?"

"If everything goes south, I just have to find a way to extricate myself without blowing up the business. You know the damage the Jarvis Thompson fiasco did. We barely survived. This has to be dealt with just right."

Claire fell back in her chair and rubbed her face, which was growing more ashen by the minute. Billy had never seen her look quite so shaken.

"I can't believe you're telling me this," she said. "I've got this tour with Ty, all these new things going, and we're short-handed without Jackson. And now, come to find out our biggest client may be a murderer."

"Again, I don't know. It's just that the possibility has recently come up. The more I'm around Russell, the more I put the pieces together, the clearer the picture becomes. He's a bad guy, and he's putting the squeeze on me."

"You should have told me before now, once you started hearing things. We're partners, remember?"

"You were heavy into what you were doing, and I guess I hoped there would be other explanations, a way out of this. We both know Russell has always walked this fine line. It started many years ago."

"Sounds like he's way over the line now."

"He wants me to come back to Orlando and nail this down with the Magic. Larry West will be shocked, to say the least. It's out of left field. He and his bosses were still grappling with the whole thing the last time I spoke with him. This won't help."

"Hell, the cops could be perp-walking Russell out of his house in handcuffs before you even get there. It'll be the lead story on the national news, and everybody will want you to comment. It's a disaster waiting to happen."

"I'll deal with it. Maybe there's a way to finesse it … we've got a lot riding on the outcome. I'm looking for answers, but I'm also going to have the ripcord in hand. I just wanted you to know."

"So Russell thinks this will all blow over and he'll be playing basketball on a big contract next season. In Orlando. It's crazy."

Billy nodded as he stood and walked slowly to the door.

"If this is true," Claire said, "I'm very concerned about our continuing involvement, even the mention of Premier in relation to Russell Mann. But I'm more concerned about you and your safety. You've been walking a fine line yourself with this kind of stuff, going back a ways. You've been lucky."

"Yeah. Lucky me." Billy flashed that bright smile and pulled the door shut behind him.

CHAPTER FORTY-SEVEN

Jackson locked up his SUV and reluctantly slid into the passenger seat of the Mercedes. Rachel took off her glasses and glanced over at him before turning the ignition and pulling away. He could feel his blood beginning to boil.

"I can't believe I'm just sitting here," Jackson said. "I'd planned on strangling you if I ever saw you again. It's what you deserve."

Rachel kept her eyes on the road and remained silent. She seemed perfectly calm under the circumstances.

"Tell me one thing: why did you have to target me? Just because you could? I wasn't involved in that. You could have gotten what you wanted some other way."

Finally, she turned toward him. "I'm sorry, Jackson. Really. I didn't used to be a vindictive person, but the last year ... I'm willing to do things I never would have done before."

"You know that Billy thinks you've lost it, and I have to agree. What did he do to you that put all this in motion? He has no idea. No one does."

Rachel slid her glasses back on and kept driving. Jackson never knew her well, but she seemed more detached from reality. She was hardly the inviting tempt-ress that had captivated him in their brief encounters.

Something had rocked her world to the point that she was willing to risk it all.

"I heard you've been hanging out with some bad people," Jackson said. "What's a rich Charleston girl doing here with a bunch of criminals in New Orleans? One day you're fine, have everything going for you, and the next day you're a different person? How does that happen? You could be working for your father or doing anything you want right now, but you're here."

"Sometimes you don't see the big picture until you step back. I had to step way back. I'm leaving soon anyway."

Jackson frowned. "Was it just the kidnapping? Billy thought the two of you were in a good place before that. What *happened* to you?"

That struck a nerve. There was a chuckle, and then outright laughter. Rachel suddenly mashed the gas and sent the Mercedes racing toward the next turn.

Jackson braced himself in the seat. *Had she lost her mind?* He wondered whether he would survive this ride or become just another casualty in a deepening mystery.

"Okay, Rachel," he said. "Please slow down." After a minute, she did.

"What *happened* to me? Billy Beckett happened to me. He was the greatest guy I ever met. And then he wasn't."

Jackson left it there. They drove on for another ten minutes in silence as the landscape grew sparser.

"Coming up," she said.

"Where? I don't trust you."

"I don't blame you, Jackson. But you got in the car. You don't have much choice at this point."

Jackson grew more nervous as he took in the changing surroundings. He had to be prepared to think and act quickly.

"You know I called Billy when I was chasing you and told him what was going on," he said. "If he doesn't hear back from me soon, he'll be coming to look for you. Or he'll let your parents know."

"What did you tell him?"

"Just that I had found you."

"Look at me, Jackson." She stopped in the middle of the road, removed her glasses again, and studied his face. "What did he say?" Her glare was withering.

Jackson stammered. "He told me to be careful and not let you get away again. That was it."

"I don't believe you. You said earlier that you didn't even know where he was."

"I was lying."

"You're lying now; Billy doesn't know you're here. Doesn't matter anyway at this point."

Rachel picked up the pace again until they passed a Dollar Tree store that sat by itself. She slowed, turned onto a secondary road and finally came to a stop, easing across the shoulder to access a long, gravel driveway. A small, brown house was barely visible in the distance. Tall trees on both sides framed it.

The house appeared to be styled after the Creole cottages that were common in the French Quarter. As they got closer, it was obvious that the place was fairly rundown. Rachel King is living *here?* Jackson worried about meeting some of her gangster friends.

Rachel pulled around back. There was a white Ford pickup parked there, and she stopped beside it and looked over at Jackson again.

"Wait," she said, and then opened her door and disappeared around the corner.

After a minute, a man with long hair and a dark beard walked slowly out the back door and approached Rachel's car. He had a handgun holstered on his hip but didn't move toward Jackson in a threatening way.

"You can come inside," he said.

Jackson walked in the back door and stopped. The living room had few furnishings and was dimly lit. Music played quietly in the background. There was no sign of Rachel.

"Have a seat," the man said, and then left the room.

CHAPTER FORTY-EIGHT

Jackson wasn't sure how much danger he was in, but he was glad to be out of the car. Rachel was growing more erratic by the minute. *What was she capable of at this point?*

Jackson even began to wonder if she might harm herself rather than him. For all he knew, she could be holding a gun to her head now, ready to pull the trigger. Or she might walk out with one pointed at him. Anything seemed possible.

He sat quietly before Rachel came in from an adjoining bedroom and took a seat beside him. She flipped off the radio. The only thing in her hand was a plain, white envelope with her first name written across it in blue ink.

"Who's your friend?" Jackson said.

"Clint. It's his place, but I come and go. He's waiting outside." Her voice sounded pleasant enough. "Don't worry."

"If you say so. Who were you visiting there in the French Quarter? Paul Romano's friends?"

"No, that time has passed. There's no reason for us to be friends anymore. I'm getting ready to leave New Orleans."

"Why did you bring me here? And please don't tell me that we're going to have more company."

"You're here because you wanted an explanation. Considering the way things have gone, maybe I do owe you one."

"You owe me more than that. Where are you going?"

"I'm not sure. Just away from here."

"You can't keep running. Your parents are hoping you'll come home."

"I know."

Jackson's eyes darted back and forth. He was drawn to a picture that was propped on a suitcase behind Rachel. It showed her standing between the Beckett brothers, everyone smiling, probably on Billy's dock down by the Tennessee River. Jackson had never seen the three of them together.

"You didn't know John, did you?" Rachel said.

He shook his head. "I used to see him sometimes when I would stop by the office, when I was still in school. He was gone by the time I was hired."

"Do you know why he died?"

"I know he shot himself at the high school baseball stadium there in Sevierville. Apparently had a lot of guilt about the kidnapping."

"He had other issues, too. Drug issues. He had felt for years like he was a failure. It all came crashing down."

"Billy never talked much about it, and I didn't ask. That was a horrible time for him and his father. For a lot of people, including you. You were involved in all that. It's how we ended up here."

Rachel stared out the window intently, as if trying to pull something painful from deep in the memory bank.

"I was at John's funeral; it's the last time I saw Billy. It was raining, a sad day. John had problems, but he was a good-hearted guy. I was with him more toward the end and got to understand him better. We finally clicked." She stopped and collected herself. "I never would have believed he'd kill himself."

"Why are you telling me this?"

"Because I want you to understand, Jackson. That's why we're here. For understanding."

"But I *don't* understand. You decided to come live with these people, thugs and criminals. You're running around in the shadows, showing up here and there. It makes no sense."

Rachel tapped the envelope nervously on the table beside her.

"You know, I was getting ready to move back to Tennessee," she said. "I thought I could help Billy heal and keep his business from going under after the kidnapping. I *wanted* to help. We had some great times together, went a lot of places. I thought I loved Billy, even though we never really spelled it out that way."

She laughed and inhaled a deep breath. "He's a bastard." She pulled a letter from the envelope and offered it to Jackson.

Hesitantly, he reached out to take it. He unfolded the two pages that had been handwritten on a legal pad and began to read:

Rachel, I never wanted to write something like this, but it's time.

I was never the man I should have been — not to my parents, not to my brother, and not to you. I enjoyed our time together and want to apologize for leaving this way. I feel like a traitor and a coward.

I never should have let things get to where they did with us, but I'm not sorry. I cared about you more than Billy ever did. Did you know he was going to ask you to marry him? I saw the ring. But he got involved with someone else and moved on like he always did with women. My brother was a user. Don't let him use you anymore.

I don't want to cause any more pain. I just thought you should know. I hope you can find peace in your life.

John

Jackson stared at Rachel with a bewildered look on his face.

"John left this for you? *A suicide note?*"

"It was with some of my belongings at Billy's house. John put it there, probably on the day he died. I didn't notice until that stuff was delivered to me later. I know he left a note for his brother, too, but it was different than this."

"So you two had a thing going? Unbelievable."

"We were only together a couple of times. It just happened."

"And Billy had no idea about any of it? This isn't right. Hell, he did everything he could to help John; I know that for a fact. John wasn't telling you the truth."

"You're a fool, Jackson. Just like me." Rachel cackled. "There's something else." She opened the drawer of an end table and pulled out a photo. There was a little girl sitting on the floor, surrounded by toys, a big smile on her face.

Rachel slapped the photo down in front of Jackson.

He shook his head. "Who is she?"

"Her name is Danielle. She's mine."

"*Yours?* And who is the father? It has to be Billy, or you wouldn't be doing these things. Where is the child?"

Rachel stood up and began to pace. Tears were streaming down her cheeks. She was losing it again.

"Your time is up," she said.

"Just like that?"

"That's right. Now you can call Billy for real. I'm not going to stop you." She offered a wry smile. "Give him my best."

"You know he's going to keep looking for you. You *and* your child."

"In the end, we all do what's in our best interest. I'm leaving New Orleans, and you're going … where? Back to Tennessee?"

"No, I'm starting a new job out west, thanks to you. I don't think our motivation is the same. You're playing a different game, Rachel."

"I'm sorry you got dragged into it."

"Really?"

Jackson looked deeply into her eyes and rubbed his chin. "How did you end up here to begin with? That never made any sense."

"I didn't plan it. I met Paul Romano in Charleston and thought he was an interesting guy. We got to be friends. He invited me to come here and visit after I left Billy's. I didn't know about his father and what they were doing until later."

"But he was a mobster. And you stayed anyway."

"I wish I hadn't. There's nothing for me here now. You can tell Billy that I've moved on, in more ways than one."

"Why don't you tell him yourself? It doesn't have to be this way."

She nodded. "I'm afraid it does. Clint will take you back to your car. Goodbye, Jackson."

CHAPTER FORTY-NINE

Billy decided to check into a hotel between the airport and Windermere. He wanted to make an abrupt departure if necessary.

Russell knew his agent was flying down to Orlando, but they had yet to speak about it. Billy had left a message and was waiting to hear back.

The agent kicked off his shoes and set his phone on the bedside table. He wasn't sure what direction this saga was about to take, or even where he hoped things would stand by the end of the day. He was still essentially working on the fly.

He planned to meet briefly with Larry West, go through the motions, just to keep the channel open. There was a good chance a deal would never get done — with the Magic or anybody else — and that figured prominently in Billy's thinking. Hope was fading. He had to be willing to bail on his client, pull that ripcord, try to land as gently as possible.

Should he just go to the Orlando police and tell them everything he knew? That's what Claire would do, but she was more pragmatic. The question kept nagging at him. Billy hated being in that position, with no good options.

His phone rang. He figured it was Russell or the Magic GM, but it was neither.

"Billy Beckett?" the caller said.

"Who wants to know?"

"This is a friend of Angel's. Remember her?"

Billy took a moment to process it. He hadn't given Angel Rivera and her disappearance much more thought in recent days. He wondered if she were still alive.

"I remember," he said. "You found her? Where is she?"

"I found your office number in her shorts. She was buried in them, out on the edge of town. Bad scene, man."

There was a long silence. "I know what happened," the man said, finally. "I know about Russell Mann; he had her killed. I want you to know that we're going to make things right. Don't have any doubts. Angel deserves that, and so do our other brothers that were killed for no reason."

"What do you mean?" Billy said.

"She was trying to shake Russell down, and that's where she went wrong. Angel got in over her head. We won't bother with that. It's about respect, settling up. Prepare yourself."

"You think I control this situation?"

"You're his agent, right? I just thought you should know, and it was easy to get your cell and give you a ring. Scary, right? Everybody's an easy target these days, especially when they do the wrong things. Russell Mann has done a lot wrong. Don't have no respect for anyone or anything, especially the little people. He's going to pay a price for that."

"Wait," Billy said. It was too late. The caller was gone.

The agent tried to reach Russell again but still got no answer. He suddenly felt like he was operating in a fog. There wasn't a clear path, and time was running out.

The phone rang again, and Billy shuddered a bit before catching his breath. "Are we still on for tomorrow?" Lawrence West asked.

"Sure. Does that work for you?"

"Maybe. My office just got a call from a local reporter claiming that Russell is going to be making an appearance downtown today. He's supposedly going to announce that he's staying in Orlando. That's the word. This reporter wanted a comment from the team."

"And you said?"

"I had no comment, because it's news to us. How about you?"

"I'll be honest with you, Larry. Russell told me that his intention was to re-sign, for all the reasons we've discussed. He enjoys playing for the Magic. But I made it clear that we still had some hurdles ahead of us. We all knew that."

"*Hurdles?* Just a few million, I'd say. We're not close to an agreement."

"That's the reason I wanted to sit down with you. For what it's worth, I haven't been invited to any parties yet. This is still an ongoing process."

"Well, we can still meet, but I don't know if there's much point at the moment. I must say it's a little awkward for me to be placed in this position, Billy. You and your client need to get on the same page."

"I apologize for that, and I'd like to sit down and discuss with you tomorrow if possible. I've been trying to reach Russell all day, but he's not answering."

West sounded irritated. "Seems like he's getting harder to keep track of. That's usually a bad sign for an agent."

"What club is hosting this party?"

"Hocus Pocus is the name. Magic fans get together there on game nights. Sounded like they were going to have several show up there today."

"I'm familiar with it. I'll see you tomorrow, and we'll try to clear the air on this. Thanks for letting me know."

Billy quickly put on his shoes and glanced in the mirror. He hardly recognized himself.

Before he could put away his phone, it rang again. Russell, finally.

"Where are you?" Billy said.

"Orlovista, at T-Bone's place. I saw you'd called a few times. I been busy."

"Too busy to talk? You know better than that. There's serious trouble brewing. I know about Angel."

"I told you not to worry about that. It's not a problem."

"I just got a call from a man who assured me it *is* a problem. Her gang friends are going to be gunning for you. And maybe me, too."

"I'm not worried about that," Russell said. "I'm in the clear. I was out of the country when that went down."

"How do you know what went down? I thought she was missing."

"Let the cops figure it out."

"Her friends found her, dead and buried. She had my office number in her shorts. The cops will eventually know. You're not in the clear, believe me."

There was a long delay before Russell responded. "This deal can't fall apart. It *won't*. I've come too far."

"I'm afraid there's not much more I can do, Russell. This is some bad shit, and it's just getting deeper. It's beyond my control."

"We'll see about that. Just come here and we'll talk. You're a smart guy … you can work out anything. I always liked that about you. I'll be waiting."

CHAPTER FIFTY

Billy screeched out of the motel parking lot and sped toward the Flophouse. He knew Russell needed to be protected, but the thought kept recurring: *Why?*

If some hoodlum killed him, maybe that would be the end of it. Billy's reputation would surely take some hits — another high-profile athlete, his client, involved in a deadly skirmish — but he would be off the hook. He wouldn't have to explain what he knew, why he didn't go to the police earlier. He could barely stomach the thought of losing more than three million dollars, but it was all but gone anyway. He could just walk away. His business would go on. Life would go on.

Foolish thoughts. Billy snapped back to reality. He gritted his teeth as he tried to work his way through heavy traffic and deal with this impending disaster.

He had stored the Orlando Police Department number on his phone earlier. There was a detective's name he was familiar with, the one who had investigated the Parramore double murder. He tapped the contact and an operator answered.

"Yes," he said, "can you give me David Stein, please?"

Four rings and the operator was back on the line. "I believe he's on scene at the moment. Can I connect you to his voicemail?"

Billy pondered the question. *What would the message be?* "No, I'll try back."

He still had the Orlovista address in his Google Maps, and he called it up. The house was only ten minutes away.

When he pulled into the driveway, he expected to see Russell's SUV. But there were no vehicles visible from the street. It looked the same as the last time — like no one lived there.

Billy parked and quickly walked around to the small garage. The padlock on the side door was open, so he turned the knob and leaned in. T-Bone's car was gone, and there was no sign of Russell.

As he walked back outside, he was startled by a large man coming toward him. It was the same man who had confronted him there previously.

"So we meet again," the man said sternly.

"That's right. Looking for Russell again."

"He'll be right back."

"And you are?"

"Reaper."

Billy had felt fortunate to walk away from the man last time, and he knew he might be pushing his luck. Reaper's demeanor instantly set off alarms; he was anxious, like he was late for an important engagement. Billy felt vulnerable outside the secluded garage. He turned toward his car.

"I'll be out front," he said.

"I don't think so," came the reply.

Billy looked back and froze. Reaper had pulled a small handgun from his waistband and was pointing it at the agent's chest.

"What are you doing?"

"You're not going anywhere. Back inside."

Billy knew if he followed the command, he might never walk out of that garage again. He had to make a desperate play.

As he passed through the doorway, he turned and slammed the door with all the force he could muster. Reaper's arm was caught; he dropped his weapon with a loud groan. Billy quickly snatched it off the floor and threw open the door.

"Get down!" he yelled, taking a step back. "Now!"

Reaper stood still and clutched the injured hand, shocked to have been disarmed in such fashion. Billy leveled the weapon at his head. Finally, Reaper complied and slowly lowered himself onto the dirt face down.

Billy pressed the gun barrel to Reaper's head, just behind his left ear, and put a knee in the small of his back. "Where is Russell?" he demanded.

Reaper laid still and didn't answer.

"You don't seem to understand. I'm trying to keep him from getting killed. For some reason, he obviously doesn't feel the same about me. Time is running out here. Where is he?"

"The club downtown. There's something going on."

"And he left you here to deal with me? Are you supposed to *kill* me?"

"You can figure that out for yourself."

"While I'm doing that, I'm guessing you're the man who killed Angel. That was a mistake."

"I don't know what you're talking about."

"We'll see. You know her friends are going to pay Russell a visit, probably sooner than later? They know what you did, how that went down. Bet Russell didn't tell you that. You're both as good as dead. We may all be."

Reaper glared straight ahead. He was through talking.

"Tell you what, Reaper. I'm going to take this piece of chain and this padlock that was on the door here and lock you up while I go into town. You're a big man and I'd appreciate you making it easy for me. If you can't do that, just know that I'd rather shoot you than fight you. The cops will understand."

Billy made him sit against a workbench with his arms behind his back. He threaded the chain around Reaper's wrists and then through one of the steel legs of the bench. Reaper grimaced; his right hand was surely broken. Billy pushed the lock closed.

"Somebody will be along to get you. May be a while. Anything else you want to tell me?"

Reaper spat out his words. "Russell should have gotten rid of you a long time ago. That's going to come back to haunt him."

"Let's hope so."

CHAPTER FIFTY-ONE

Billy frowned when he heard the local sports blurb on the radio: the Orlando Magic will retain their star forward. Terms of the new deal to be announced later. No comment from Magic officials.

The agent shook his head, and he was sure Lawrence West was doing the same about now. This was foolishness; there was no deal. More head shaking to come.

Hocus Pocus was reportedly going to host a fan appreciation party in the parking lot that afternoon tied to Russell's decision and to celebrate a playoff run. Consolation prizes. Orlando didn't usually have much to trumpet at the end of the basketball season, and the fans would take what they could get.

The gathering was public knowledge now. Billy wondered who else might be tuned in. He was afraid to know.

He was back in the Milk District within minutes. There was a lot of traffic around the club as he passed, and Billy could see a bar had been set up in the parking lot. Several patrons were milling around, talking and waiting to catch a glimpse of the guest of honor.

By the time Billy found a parking spot and walked back, a small crowd had gathered. A couple of news reporters waited impatiently for their remote broadcasts. For all intents and purposes, it was a chance for the fans to get close to a famous player, have a drink and some free hors d'oeuvres, and soak up a few rays.

Billy stood back and surveyed the scene. Russell was getting the attention he wanted.

After a couple of minutes, a white Range Rover limousine stopped at the curb. The driver stepped out in a crisp blue suit and opened a passenger door. Russell unfolded those long legs and emerged. He was wearing dark sunglasses, white shorts and sneakers, and a blue Magic t-shirt. The two men Billy had seen there with T-Bone weeks earlier were right behind him.

The Hocus Pocus owner and his manager greeted the group and steered Russell into the club while his friends stood watch. He would come back out when the stage was set.

Billy kept his distance. In that moment, he couldn't help but think about how far the dream had advanced — the deeply troubled kid from the big city, the longest of shots, rising near the top of the basketball world, on the verge of unimaginable wealth — only to crash and burn. And the worst part: the agent couldn't do a damn thing to stop it.

The last thought was the one that lingered in Billy's mind. He had failed in his duty, and it was going to cost him. Without a little luck, taking on Russell might have already been a fatal mistake.

Russell probably thought Billy was out of the way by now. One fewer witness against him. No doubt he would be surprised when his agent showed up to join the festivities.

The Florida air was heating up. Billy paced on the sidewalk in a bit of a daze as the Magic theme song began to play on the big speakers. The fans moved toward an area that had been roped off near the bar.

There was Russell with a broad smile and the typical air of invincibility as he walked across in front of the cheering crowd and stopped. The chatter died down.

"I just want everybody to know that the rise of Russell Mann will continue — in Orlando," he said, raising his arms in a warm embrace. "Nothing official yet, but here's the secret: I've decided to re-sign with the Magic." There were cheers all around. "Gonna win a championship next season — I guarantee it." More applause. "Thanks for your support, and enjoy this little party. It's on me."

The music resumed and fans converged on the all-star to slap hands and offer encouragement. A radio personality leaned in with a microphone. Russell beamed.

Billy decided to get in line with the others and slowly approach his client. Russell didn't notice him until Billy was close enough to be heard. The look on his face said it all.

"Congratulations," Billy said. "I'm ready to talk now. Are *you?*"

Russell's shoulders slumped; he was unnerved. He pointed to the side of the bar, and they walked around behind it, out of earshot. His bodyguards kept a nervous watch.

"Billy ... I ..."

"You *what?* Didn't think I'd make it? Where did you think I'd be? With Reaper?"

"Sorry, man, but change of plans. I couldn't stay … he was supposed to tell you. Where is he?"

"Oh, he told me, before he ran into a little trouble. I imagine he's still chained up in the garage. I took his gun away from him and left him there."

Russell exhaled deeply and his expression turned grim. He looked like a man who had finally been cornered after a long, exhausting chase.

"You didn't expect to see me again, did you?" Billy said. "You left Reaper there to take me out. After all I've done for you."

"It's not like that."

"You had it all, and you threw it away. For nothing. I tried to help you, hung with you through thick and thin. You said it yourself: I believed in you when nobody else would. What was your next move, Russell? Did you think you'd just keep going, even after I was out of the picture? It's over."

"Billy, we need to talk."

"That's what you said earlier and it almost got me killed. I'll be talking all right — to the police. And I'm sure they'll want to talk to you. I expect to see them here any minute, in fact."

Russell turned quickly and started to walk away. He didn't get far.

From out of the crowd there was a gunshot, and then another. The first round had whizzed past Billy's head and lodged in the wood fence behind him. He dropped to the ground as the panicked crowd scattered.

Another shot came from a different direction, and the assailant went down. One of Russell's bodyguards stood over the man as he lay motionless and bleeding heavily.

A couple of police officers that had been nearby quickly moved in with their weapons drawn. The bodyguard dropped his gun and raised his hands. After a few frantic seconds, the shooting was over. The sirens wailed as more officers arrived to secure the chaotic scene.

Billy was finally able to collect himself and survey the damage.

Russell Mann was being tended to on the ground. He had suffered a gaping chest wound, and there was a look of disbelief in his eyes. In all his close calls through the years, he actually had never been *hit* before.

He struggled to breathe. Emergency personnel scrambled to stabilize him as he was placed on a stretcher, still wide-eyed, and rolled to a waiting ambulance. The hospital was just a few minutes away.

Russell had wanted to be the man of the hour, the toast of the town, and he got more than he bargained for. This news would rock Orlando and the basketball world for many days to come.

Billy stood among a group of stunned witnesses and waited to talk to detectives. He wasn't even sure where to begin.

CHAPTER FIFTY-TWO

The interview with Detective Stein and his partner went on for more than three hours, and Billy was exhausted when he walked out of the building. He knew it was only the beginning. There would be follow-up interviews in the coming days and weeks. The bad publicity was coming.

The agent was only starting to realize what a tangled web Russell had spun, and how he had been caught up in it. *How did an NBA star get so far off track? He really did believe he was invincible.* There were mixed emotions, all bubbling to the surface.

In one sense, Billy felt relief. Russell Mann wasn't his problem anymore. Sure, it was a costly lesson. Very costly. But the agent could have been killed trying to do what was right. He had survived.

In another sense, there was just disappointment — in himself, mostly. He hadn't seen disaster coming soon enough to head it off. Or he thought he could somehow mitigate it. His instincts had let him down. It was the kind of disappointment that would linger.

The Orlando Police Department headquarters was a new state-of-the-art facility, a stylish glass and steel structure with a public plaza and sculptures. It wasn't like any police station Billy had ever been in.

He took a seat on a bench outside the building and checked his phone. He knew Claire would be breathlessly awaiting the details. He had sent her a text message earlier but got nothing back.

He pressed the phone against his cheek. "Well, I'm out of jail," he said. "At least for now."

She startled him with her quick response. "I'm here."

Billy looked around and saw her walking toward him, across the courtyard. They met in a long embrace. Claire was there. Again. When it mattered most.

"You didn't tell me you were coming," Billy said. "You didn't need to do that. I've got this under control."

"I can tell. When I first heard what was going on, I knew you'd be in the middle of it. Don Woodall offered to have his pilot fly me down in the spur of the moment." She looked deeply into Billy's eyes. "I'm glad to see you're all right."

"Not all right, exactly. But okay."

"I've been sitting here waiting and watching the news. It's pretty bad — cringe worthy, I'd say. Congratulations on not getting yourself killed. That's the only bright spot I can see."

Billy managed a wry smile. "I said I'd try to get us out without blowing up the business. Hear any bombs land in Knoxville before you left?"

"No," she said, "but it's still early. We're going to have a rough few weeks ahead. Russell left a trail of — what was it you called it? *Criminality?* And we probably don't know the half of it yet. He was everything we feared, and more."

"At this point, I feel foolish for being sucked in." He shook his head. "I thought I could manage it."

"That relationship started a long time ago. We knew the potential trouble with Russell, but sometimes you have to take a chance in this business. A lot of times. He's a hell of a talent; there's no denying that. I agreed that he seemed to be worth the risk."

"Thanks for trying to make me feel better," Billy said, "but this is all on *me*. Weighing risk versus reward with clients is one of the things I do best." He took a deep breath. "Not this time."

"They're saying Russell is in critical condition. The guy who shot him supposedly was a member of one of the gangs downtown. He's dead."

"Yeah, I heard."

"What now?"

"I'm going to stay over tonight and see where things go. I'm sure the cops are combing through Russell's place, and Detective Stein wanted me to stay available. I assume they've already picked up his friend in the garage. That guy's likely involved in all sorts of stuff. He was supposed to make me disappear."

"This is crazy, Billy, way beyond your job description. You really pushed your luck. I didn't know if I was going to find you dead or alive today."

"I'm sorry you felt like you needed to come. But thanks. It means a lot."

She scowled at him. "We *are* partners, so we're in this together. I just didn't fully appreciate how deep you'd gotten yourself this time."

"I told you."

"A little late. And I was very concerned, if you'll recall. I knew it was bad and likely to get worse, but I didn't expect *this*."

"I'll handle it from here, Claire."

"If you say so. While I'm here, I've got a little advance work I can do for Ty's tour. There are a couple of contacts I want to talk to in Orlando."

"So *that's* the real reason you came? Always taking care of Ty Nelson." She smiled. "You're planning to do the Florida gigs with him?"

"At least the first couple. He wants me to come to Nashville and discuss things here in the next few days."

"You guys are getting pretty close."

"Trying to go slow on the personal front. I'm really afraid to get too involved, blur the lines. That's not good for business."

"I've heard it can happen," Billy said with a sarcastic smile. "You just go on and don't worry about me. It's probably best for you to be out of the office anyway for the next little bit. I'll be back as soon as I can to handle all the incoming fire. I'll call Candace and tell her what's going on; she'll be thrilled. Why don't we get together later? I could use a drink or ten."

Billy looked around at all the people coming and going. He noticed David Stein walk out of the building headed toward the parking lot.

"Come with me," he said, motioning for Claire to follow. They intercepted Stein before he got to his car. "Detective, this is my business partner, Claire Bosken." Stein nodded. "I just wondered if your men found Reaper in the garage in Orlovista."

"Actually, no. He was gone, but we're looking for him. There is one other thing, Mr. Beckett."

"What is it?"

"It's Russell Mann. He just died."

CHAPTER FIFTY-THREE

Jackson was all the way to California when he decided to make the call. He wanted to unburden himself before moving on with his life. He had a scheduled meeting with his new business partners in Los Angeles, and then would head north to Seattle.

His mind had been racing since he left Rachel, more than fifteen hundred miles ago. *Why had she shown him the letter? And the picture? Who was the father of the child? What did any of it prove? Was she just messing with his head again?* He couldn't keep the thoughts to himself any longer.

On the other side of the country, Billy was sitting in a bar near his Orlando motel. He had just sent Claire on her way, after a little Jack Daniel's sedative, and he did a double take when the phone rang.

"Jackson?"

There was a momentary lapse as Jackson braced himself for the conversation. It wasn't unusual for them to talk at least twice a day when they worked together, discuss any number of topics, but those times seemed distant now. He wasn't sure he'd ever hear Billy's voice again. Hopefully it was the right thing to do.

"Listen, Billy, I'm sorry to bother you," he said. "I'm sure you don't want to hear from me again, and I don't blame you. I'm just driving and..."

"Where are you?"

"In California. Got a meeting in L.A. before heading up to Seattle. I've been doing a lot of thinking. I need to tell you something."

"Should I order another drink first?"

"What do you mean?"

"Never mind; it's been a long day. I'm in Orlando, and Claire just left. Go ahead."

Jackson didn't want to hurt Billy again. There was no one he respected more. Billy had been his mentor, his role model. He was still feeling the pain of their falling out deep in his gut.

Should he even go down this road? He had no choice.

"I saw Rachel again," he blurted out. "In New Orleans."

The sigh on the other end was audible. "Let's don't go there, Jackson. I'm still trying to get over our last conversation about her."

"I know, and I couldn't be sorrier. I just thought you should be aware of what Rachel told me. I don't know how much is true, but you can do whatever you want with the information. Take it for what it's worth."

"I'm waiting."

Jackson took a deep breath. "When I left Knoxville," he said, "I decided to go down and see if I could find her. I had a few days before I needed to be out here and thought, What the hell? I talked to some people in New Orleans and had a general idea where she might be."

Billy interrupted. "Hasn't she caused you enough grief? All of us?"

"I know. I just haven't been able to get this out of my mind ... it was surreal. I thought maybe now I could be of some help."

"Keep going, Jackson."

"I went to an area where Rachel supposedly hung out in the French Quarter. This bartender had seen her around. Amazingly, I ended up finding her and chasing her down. I told her it was time to come clean, put an end to all this. She wanted me to get in her car so she could show me something."

"And you did?"

"It was freaky. She drove me to one of the places she's been staying. We talked ... her mind is pretty scattered. Totally different person than the one you used to know. Her time down there has changed her, and not for the better."

"Was she alone?"

"There was a guy at this cottage out on the edge of New Orleans, but I think he just owned the place and let her stay there when she wanted. Maybe he's one of Romano's leftovers. He didn't have much to say when he drove me back to my car."

"Her father and I beat the bushes when we were there, too, but didn't get anywhere. I think Rachel was still running around with some mafia types. We figured they were protecting her."

"She said she'd put all that behind her; she was alone when I caught up to her. It was a strange couple of hours after that. I left with more questions than answers. Maybe you can find the answers."

"Okay. Tell me what you know."

"First, she started talking about John. That seemed strange."

"John?"

"There was a picture there in the house. It was you and her and your brother — the three of you posing together, maybe down on your dock. I guess she had kept it with her."

"I'm familiar with it. I thought it was still at *my* house. What did she say?"

"She talked about being at John's funeral, how she couldn't believe he's gone. Later she admitted that they had, uh, gotten together a couple of times before he died."

"What?"

"I know it's painful to hear now, and I debated whether to tell you, whether it was true or mattered anyway at this point."

"Rachel and my brother?" There was another heavy sigh on the line. "They were working together, but I never imagined that. Apparently this is my day to feel like an absolute fool. What made you decide that it mattered to me?"

There was another long pause. "She pulled a picture out of a drawer there. And again, I don't know, Billy."

"Go on."

"It was a picture of a little girl. Just sitting on the floor somewhere, smiling. Rachel said her name is Danielle. *Her daughter.* I asked who the father was and she wouldn't tell me. She wouldn't tell me where the child was either. I didn't see any evidence that one had been staying there at the house."

Jackson could tell that Billy was trying to process all this. He waited.

Billy spoke haltingly. "I stopped in Charleston to see her parents. It was a few days after you left my house, and I wanted to ask Bradley about your suspicions. He finally admitted knowing that Rachel was pregnant before she left, but he claimed not to know anything more. She was supposedly stressed out and wanted to clear her head. She never came back."

"And he didn't know the father?"

"No, and he said she didn't know either at the time." The angst was building. "I can't believe we spent three days together looking for Rachel, and Bradley didn't say a word to me about it. None of it."

"Everything about this is bizarre. At the end, Rachel said she was leaving New Orleans, so there was no need to look for her there again. She wanted me to tell you that. I told her she ought to go home, or just come talk to you, but I don't think she was listening."

"So what you're saying, Jackson, is that Rachel has a daughter out there somewhere. She may be mine, she may be my brother's, she may be Paul Romano's. Hell, she may be somebody else's. And we have no idea where she is."

"There's more, unfortunately. I saw a letter John had written to Rachel before his death. It mentioned you supposedly buying a ring for Rachel but never asking her to marry you. He specifically said you deserved to be hurt because you didn't care about either of them."

"That's ridiculous; I tried everything to help John. He wasn't in his right mind at the end. I know that for a fact."

"I told Rachel the same thing, but she wasn't buying it. She obviously has been stewing over this for a while."

"And that's why she's been stalking me all these months? Because I didn't ask her to marry me? The ring was a bad idea; I still have it. I never should have shown it to John. He promised me he'd never say anything. Why would he send that letter?"

"Like I said, I'm sorry to be the one to lay this on you. I know you don't want to hear any of it, but I had to call."

Billy was willing to let the conversation die there. "You did the right thing, Jackson," he said wistfully. "I hope things work out for you. For all of us."

Jackson could feel the pain welling up inside again. "Good luck. I'll be thinking about you."

CHAPTER FIFTY-FOUR

The dust stirred up by the rise and fall of Russell Mann was beginning to settle.

Orlando police already had a better understanding of what had gone on behind the scenes with the Magic star. They had begun to put together a timeline of the crimes, spoken with law enforcement colleagues in New York, local gang members, team officials. The player's properties in Windermere and Orlovista had been searched. In short order, the dots of his past were being connected. It wasn't a pretty picture.

The Orlando community, in particular, was still reeling from the news. In the history of the NBA, there had never been anything quite like it. The Magic couldn't have asked for worse publicity.

Billy spent the morning talking again with Detective Stein, just to clarify several details in the building case. The detective's parting comment stuck with him: "You're going to be tied to this for a while, but life goes on. That's not the case for some others." Billy was free to leave.

The man called Reaper was still missing, but police were on his trail. They knew his real name, David Murray, and were beginning to contact acquaintances in his hometown of Kissimmee, just south of Orlando. Given the media attention the case was drawing, it was only a matter of time before he was found.

The drive up the East Coast to Isle of Palms, South Carolina was about six hours, and the end was in sight. Billy was anxious to get there. He had jumped off I-95 just beyond Coosawhatchie and taken state route 17 east toward Charleston. A short drive on the I-526 connector left him in Mount Pleasant, fifteen minutes from the King mansion, late on a sunny, breezy afternoon.

Billy could feel the draw of the Lowcountry tugging at him again. The allure never went away, but the days when he and Rachel vacationed together on the slender barrier island seemed long ago.

Bradley and Elaine King were expecting him. He had given them a couple hours notice and told them briefly about Jackson's encounter with Rachel. Nothing about the sequence of events was clear in Billy's mind.

He was greeted at the door by Bradley, who was cordial but short. "Come in." The men walked through the house and out to the gazebo in the back. They took a seat in the shade. Elaine joined them with a pitcher of iced tea a minute later.

"Hello, Billy," Elaine said, forcing a smile. "Here you are again."

"I hope we're close to getting a handle on things this time," Billy said. "It feels like it, for some reason."

Bradley spoke up. "I'm sorry for what you've been through in Orlando. We've been watching. Seems like there's a lot of pain to go around these days. It never ends."

"No shortage of that, for sure."

"How are you doing?"

"I could be better. A lot better. So many thoughts are swimming around in my head. I need answers."

Elaine, ever the Southern belle, stood and poured everyone a glass of sweet tea. "We understand," she said. "Go ahead."

"As I told you on the phone, Jackson had spoken with Rachel in New Orleans, and a lot of different things started coming together. I know there's a child in the picture now — your grandchild. A little girl. You're aware of that?"

"Yes, Danielle. She had been staying with us."

"*Here?* Where was she the last time I sat in this very spot?"

The Kings looked at each other regretfully. Neither wanted to speak. "She was here," Elaine said, "but she isn't now."

"Why didn't you tell me? I've been in the middle of all this from the start, trying to understand. Trying to *help.* Don't you think I deserve to know the truth? I can't believe you'd keep something like that from me."

Bradley took a deep breath and looked at his wife. "Elaine wanted to tell you. We didn't know the truth then. We just had Dani."

"Dani, huh? You know the truth now? Am I the father? And where is she?"

The sliding door to the terrace suddenly opened. Rachel stood with her daughter in her arms.

There was a grim look on her face as she stared out at her parents and former lover. Billy felt a jolt, like the wind had just been knocked out of him.

Rachel slowly approached them, her eyes focused squarely on Billy. He tried to comprehend what was happening and spoke at a whisper.

"Rachel."

Elaine came to her side and took Danielle. She nodded to Bradley. "We'll leave you and Billy alone," she said.

CHAPTER FIFTY-FIVE

The Kings walked silently into the house. Rachel and Billy were finally together again.

After all this time, he wasn't sure where to begin. He could only shake his head and mutter. *"Why?"* So many questions all rolled into one.

Rachel looked into Billy's eyes, searching for something, and then turned away and walked to the railing. When they lived together, he used to accuse her of gazing into the distance, beyond the Tennessee River, for a connection whenever the subject got uncomfortable or complicated. Now she stared out at the Atlantic, the refuge of her youth.

"I wasn't sure I'd see you again," she said.

"Seems you were doing everything in your power to keep from it. Again, why?"

She pursed her lips. "I don't like you, Billy. That much I've learned."

"What happened? You just left and never came back. What did I do to you?"

"I'm not sure how to answer that."

"Jackson told me what you said. I couldn't believe it. Any of it. John was feeding you a line, right to the end."

"You didn't buy me a ring? You didn't love me?"

"That wasn't it."

Billy looked away and rubbed his face. Rachel started to leave, but he gently squeezed her arm and stopped her. He pulled out a chair and motioned for her to sit. Reluctantly she did.

"Help me understand," he said. "Why didn't you just come to me? We had some bad times, but we could usually talk things out. I worried about you, even after finding out you had gone to New Orleans to be with Paul Romano. Why?"

"I was confused and angry. The pressure built during the kidnapping and I lost it. I felt like I lost everything."

"But you were there, with one of the men responsible for that whole plot. You decided to be with him instead of me. It still blows me away to think about it. There's no excuse."

"It was a terrible mistake. And then I was alone."

"So why be angry with me? Because of the letter John wrote you?"

She nodded and quietly began to sob.

"Let's just be clear here," Billy said. "You're the one who was sleeping around behind my back. With my brother, for God's sake. And with this two-bit mobster. You almost ruined me and my business. Hell, you almost got me killed. I shouldn't even be talking to you."

"What about the other women? Holly?"

"*Holly?* She had nothing to do with this. Weren't you the one who said we weren't really in love, that you didn't want to get in too deep? You made it a point, right here in this very house. We were just having a good time, enjoying each other's company. I thought that's the way you wanted it. And then things got complicated — and very dark."

He took a deep breath and exhaled. "Is Danielle mine? That's the reason I'm here."

Rachel's lips quivered and she stared out at the ocean again. "No."

"I don't believe you."

"I knew you'd say that." She pulled papers from her purse. "Here are the results of the paternity test. She's not your child."

He sat motionless for a minute as he scanned the pages. "How did you get a DNA sample?"

"Jackson helped me. He didn't realize what he was doing."

Billy stood and walked away. He wasn't sure how to process this. "The summary says I'm not the father but it can't rule out a relative."

"That's right. She's John's." Rachel took a deep breath. "I haven't known long. I'm still trying to grasp it."

"So Danielle is my *niece?*" Billy raked his fingers through his hair.

"I wanted her to be yours, but I was afraid when I found out I was pregnant. I was going to come to you. When I got John's letter, saw that you had been ready to marry me and then … I wanted to hurt you. That feeling has only grown."

"You've succeeded, Rachel. You had your own affairs. You walked out on me, coerced Jackson. Hell, you were living with *mobsters.* I've had many sleepless nights thinking about you, been with your father to look for you. And now to find out Danielle is the daughter of my dead brother. You've hurt me more than you'll ever know."

Billy slumped in his chair and rubbed his face. "I don't know where to go from here."

"I could say I'm sorry, but there's something inside that still isn't sure. I hope I can become a different person, a better person. Maybe just feel normal again. I've put New Orleans and that part of my life behind me. I'm going to be staying here with my parents for a while."

"You need to get some treatment, for your daughter's sake if nothing else. Your parents will help you if you let them."

Billy stood and turned to leave. Rachel was still the most intriguing woman he had ever known, but he knew they had no future together. They both knew.

"Goodbye, Rachel," he said.

She stood still, her dark hair blowing in the breeze, before turning back toward the ocean.

CHAPTER FIFTY-SIX

Billy was eager to see his father. The most recent medical report had been encouraging, a ray of hope in an otherwise depressing prognosis.

Franklin had taken a leave of absence from work. He looked better, more energetic, than the last time his son had seen him. He was able to stand and give Billy a hearty hug when he walked into the house. His stoic sense of humor was still intact.

"I see that you're at it again," Franklin said. "Aren't there better ways to make the national news?"

"I always wanted to be famous."

"Infamous is more like it. That's two of your clients now who have strayed into that territory, far from the sports pages. At least Jarvis Thompson lived through it. Sounded like Russell Mann got what he had coming."

"I hate it. Russell wasn't dealt a very good hand in life, and he didn't play it like Jarvis. He went the other direction. But I could have done more. I *should* have done more."

"I'm sorry to keep going back to it," Franklin said, "but I told you a long time ago that you'd be better off if you'd stayed in corporate law. It's safer. Boring, but safe."

Billy laughed. "But not as interesting, right? Let's just leave it at that for the moment."

They went into the den and settled on the couch. Franklin said his cancer treatments had been going well. He was upbeat.

He was defying the odds, just as those who knew him would have expected. He'd always been a fighter.

"So tell me how you're really feeling," Billy said. "The honest truth."

"It just depends. Some days not too bad. It doesn't help when I hear you're out trying to get yourself killed. What the hell happened down there?"

"Long story, and we'll talk more later. For now, I just want to tell you something else you don't know. Jackson found Rachel down in New Orleans."

The news perked Franklin right up. "Rachel? Is she all right?"

"I think she's all right; I've seen her. There are some things I need to discuss with you, and they may surprise you. They definitely surprised me."

"Okay."

Billy braced himself for another tough conversation. "Turns out Rachel and John were closer than we knew. They shared some intimate moments before he left us."

The news caused Franklin to cock his head and narrow his eyes. He kept listening.

"They were together a lot toward the end. I'll take part of the blame for not keeping a closer eye of the situation. They were working for me."

"I hate to hear that, son," Franklin said. "It just adds to the pain, I know."

"I don't guess I should be surprised by anything at this point. John also wrote Rachel a letter. He said he was sorry for letting things get out of hand between them, but he also accused me of not caring about either one of them."

"That's not true, Billy."

"No, but it still hurts. We spent a lot of good years together, all of us." He was fighting back tears. "It was bad enough to lose Mother, because of me and my carelessness. And then to have everything come apart at the end with John like it did..."

"It's not your fault," Franklin said. "I keep telling you that. Things happen in life that you don't plan for. You just have to keep going, do the best you can. I'm still trying to learn that myself."

Billy managed a smile. "I'm not sure I'll make it if something happens to you. You have to keep fighting with everything you've got."

"You can count on it, son."

"That's what I like to hear. And so I'm hoping to give you a little extra motivation today."

"How so?"

Billy went to the front door and waved. He opened the storm door and in walked Claire, holding a little girl. Billy took the child, and the three of them slowly approached Franklin.

"This is Danielle, Dad. She's your granddaughter."

Franklin was speechless at first as he tried to understand. He then reached out, and Billy placed the girl in his arms. She had dark hair and hazel eyes, like her mother, and a bright smile came over her immediately.

"She's John's," Billy said.

"I can't believe it." Franklin brought her closer to his face and studied her carefully. His eyes were misty. "Hello, sweetheart. Maybe I can see it a little more now. She looks like a Beckett."

"She does," Claire said. "Beautiful."

Billy just stood quietly beside them.

"What about Rachel?" Franklin said. "Where is she?"

"She's at a hotel down the road here," Billy said. "She let us bring Danielle for you to meet; you know Rachel always liked you a lot. She'll be going back to Charleston. Her parents are waiting anxiously, hoping to make up for lost time."

Franklin nodded. He held Danielle for a few more minutes and then gave her back to Billy. "She's a gorgeous child. Thank you for bringing her, and thank Rachel. I know she's going through some very difficult times. I can't imagine what John would say. I only wish he were here."

Franklin grimaced slightly as he lowered himself back to the couch. The emotional release was taking a toll, but he was happy.

Billy walked to the door and paused. He stared at his father while Claire stepped outside.

"I'm sorry, son," Franklin said.

"Me, too, Dad."

Billy pulled the girl tight to his chest and left without another word.

###

Thank you for reading, and I sincerely hope you enjoyed *Ripcord*. As an independently published author, I rely on you, the reader, to spread the word. So if you enjoyed the book, please tell your friends and family, and if it isn't too much trouble, I would appreciate a brief review on Amazon. Thanks again. My best to you and yours.

-Scott

ABOUT THE AUTHOR

Scott Pratt was born in South Haven, Michigan, and moved to Tennessee when he was thirteen years old. He was a veteran of the United States Air Force and held a Bachelor of Arts degree in English from East Tennessee State University and a Doctor of Jurisprudence from the University of Tennessee College of Law. He lived in Northeast Tennessee until his untimely death in November, 2018.

www.scottprattfiction.com

ALSO BY SCOTT PRATT

An Innocent Client (Joe Dillard #1)
In Good Faith (Joe Dillard #2)
Injustice for All (Joe Dillard #3)
Reasonable Fear (Joe Dillard #4)
Conflict of Interest (Joe Dillard #5)
Blood Money (Joe Dillard #6)
A Crime of Passion (Joe Dillard #7)
Judgment Cometh (And That Right Soon) (Joe Dillard #8)
Due Process (Joe Dillard #9)
Justice Redeemed (Darren Street #1)
Justice Burning (Darren Street #2)
Justice Lost (Darren Street #3)
River on Fire
The Sins of the Mother w/ Mark
Stout (Miller & Stevens #1)

ABOUT THE AUTHOR

Kelly Hodge is a native of Johnson City, Tennessee. He graduated from East Tennessee State University with majors in communications and political science, and spent more than three decades in the newspaper industry as a writer and editor. He lives in the beautiful mountains of Northeast Tennessee

www.kellyhodge.squarespace.com

ALSO BY KELLY HODGE

Deep Threat (Billy Beckett #1)
Divine Strike (Billy Beckett #2)